Enchanting Tales

for young readers

THIS IS A PARRAGON BOOK

© Parragon 1998

Parragon
13 Whiteladies Road, Clifton, Bristol BS8 1PB

Produced by
The Templar Company plc,
Pippbrook Mill, London Road, Dorking,
Surrey RH4 1JE

Printed in Italy

ISBN 0 75252 836 X

Illustrated by:
Diana Catchpole, Robin Edmonds, Paul Gamble, Phil Garner, Claire Mumford,
Jenny Press, Lesley Smith, Jane Taylor

Enchanting Tales

for young readers

PARRAGON

This book belongs to

. . . .

Contents

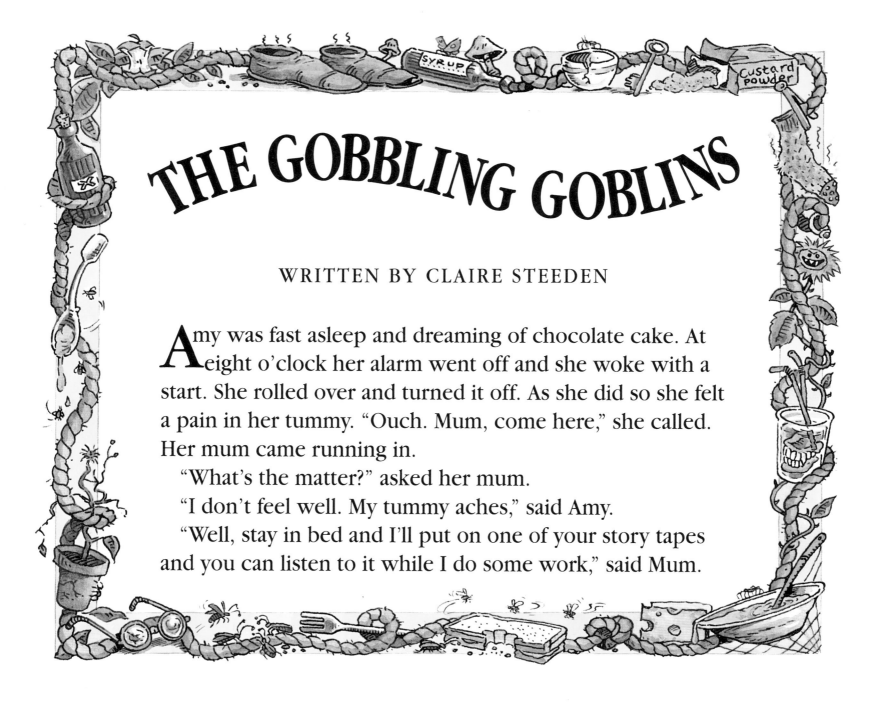

THE GOBBLING GOBLINS

WRITTEN BY CLAIRE STEEDEN

Amy was fast asleep and dreaming of chocolate cake. At eight o'clock her alarm went off and she woke with a start. She rolled over and turned it off. As she did so she felt a pain in her tummy. "Ouch. Mum, come here," she called. Her mum came running in.

"What's the matter?" asked her mum.

"I don't feel well. My tummy aches," said Amy.

"Well, stay in bed and I'll put on one of your story tapes and you can listen to it while I do some work," said Mum.

Amy snuggled into her duvet listening to a story about goblins, and gazing at the doll's house in the corner of her room. After a while she felt sleepy, but as she began to doze she thought she saw two little faces looking out through her doll's house window. She woke again later, when her mum came into the room. "How are you feeling?" asked Mum.

"I still feel a bit poorly. I just had a funny dream about goblins living in my doll's house," said Amy.

"There aren't any goblins in your doll's house, silly," laughed Mum.

"I wish there were. It would be fun," said Amy.

"No it wouldn't. Goblins are usually very naughty," said Mum. "Are you hungry? Would you like some lunch?"

"Not really," mumbled Amy.

"Well, how about a nice boiled egg with soldiers?" suggested Mum.

Amy followed her mum downstairs and lay on the sofa watching television while mum made lunch.

"Eat up," said Mum, as she set down a tray in front of Amy.

"But I don't feel very hungry," whined Amy.

"How about if I help you?" asked Mum, and she dipped the spoon into the egg. "O.K.," smiled Amy.

Just as the spoon got close to Amy's mouth, the phone rang and her Mum turned away to answer it. Amy was about to eat the egg when two goblins ran out from behind the salt and pepper pots, jumped up and ate all the egg off the spoon. Amy could not believe her eyes! They looked just like the goblins in her dream. They ran back to their hiding place, giggling.

Amy's Mum put the phone down, turned back to Amy and looked at the spoon.

"So you are hungry after all," said Mum.

"I didn't eat it. It was the goblins hiding behind the pepper pot," said Amy, pointing to the tray. "Didn't you see them?"

"No," said Mum. "You and your goblins. Let's get on with lunch."

"But I'm not hungry," said Amy.

"Well, you soon gobbled the last spoonful. I know, if I look away maybe the goblins will eat it again," laughed Mum. She was happy to play Amy's game if it meant she ate her lunch. So she dipped a soldier into the egg, held it in front of Amy, and looked away.

Amy sat and stared in amazement as again the goblins dashed out, ate the food and ran back.

Amy started to giggle because they looked so funny. Mum turned back and saw that the soldier had gone.

"Who could have eaten that?" asked Mum with a smile.

"The goblins ate it," laughed Amy.

"They must be hungry. Let's give them some more," said mum. Amy and her mum sat on the sofa playing this game while the goblins ran back and forth eating Amy's lunch, until it was all gone. "That was fun," said Amy.

"Good," said Mum. "Lie here and watch television, and you'll soon start to feel better now you've eaten." As Mum left the room the goblins crept out and called to Amy. "Psstt, thanks for lunch."

"That's all right. I wasn't hungry. Where did you come from?" asked Amy.

"Oh, we live in a lovely little house upstairs," replied the goblins.

"What! In my doll's house? So it *was* your faces I saw at the window!" said Amy.

"Who are you talking to?" asked Mum coming back into the room.

"The goblins," answered Amy. "Look!" She pointed to where the goblins had been, but they had dived behind a cushion when they heard Mum coming.

"I think you've been dreaming again," said Mum.

Amy lay on the sofa watching T.V., but after a while she felt hungry, and asked her mum for something to eat.

" You can't feel hungry after eating all that lunch," said Mum.

"But I didn't eat any lunch. The goblins did," whined Amy.

"Don't be silly. That was only a game."

"But they *did* eat it. They came downstairs from my doll's house," Amy explained.

"You've been having lots of funny dreams this morning while you've been poorly. There are no such things as goblins," laughed Mum.

"There are. They're real. I saw them. And they ate my lunch and now I'm hungry," said Amy.

"I think you'd better go upstairs to your room. I know that you're not feeling well but that's no excuse for telling lies. You can have something to eat later," said Mum.

"That's not fair," cried Amy. She slowly climbed the stairs, laid down on her bed and started to cry. Munch and Crunch, the goblins, looked out from the doll's house and saw Amy was upset. They ran out and jumped onto Amy's bed.

"What's the matter? Do you still feel poorly?" they asked.

"No," sobbed Amy. "I feel much better, but I'm hungry and Mum won't believe that you ate my lunch."

"Grown-ups!" sighed Munch.

"We're very sorry. But it seemed a shame to waste it. We didn't mean to get you into trouble. " said Crunch.

"Never mind," said Amy. "It's not your fault."

"But it is," said Munch. "So we'll make it up to you. Wait a minute."

Munch whispered something to Crunch and they jumped down onto the floor and dashed into the doll's house. Amy sat and waited, but not for long. Soon Munch and Crunch came running out with trays filled with all the plastic food from the doll's house kitchen.

"I can't eat that," laughed Amy, "it's not real."

"Of course you can eat it," said Munch. "Watch."

With that Munch and Crunch held hands and started jumping up and down. As they did so they called out,

"Plastic food, you look so yummy. Become real, to fill my tummy."

With that there was a bright flash, and when Amy opened her eyes there in front of her was a real feast! "Oh, wow," she cried. "Thank you." Amy tucked into sandwiches, cakes, crisps, sausage rolls, biscuits and ice cream. After a while she said, "I'm full. I can't eat any more. Thank you." "We'd better clear up before your mum comes," said Crunch.

With another flash all the food vanished.

"We'd better go. Sorry you got into trouble, but I hope you enjoyed our lunch," said Crunch.

"Oh, I did. It was much nicer than a boiled egg," said Amy and they all laughed. They said goodbye and in a flash the goblins had gone.

Amy was just licking the last bit of ice cream from her lips when Mum came in with a tray of food.

"I thought that you might want some tea and biscuits," said Mum.

"Yes please," said Amy.

Mum sat on the bed and gave Amy the tray. Just then the phone rang and mum went to answer it. When she came back all the biscuits had gone.

"Who ate all those?" asked Mum.

"I did," replied Amy. "The goblins have gone home."

NED THE GNOME

WRITTEN BY AMBER HUNT

Ned the Gnome spent the morning sticking his feet into icky sticky mud puddles and breathing deeply the horrible smell that accompanies icky sticky mud. He tried to tell himself he loved the mud and adored the smell, but he didn't, not really … not even a little bit. Eventually, feeling quite down in the dumps, Ned went and sat on the top of a little hill, wondering what he was going to do.

"Excuse me," said a voice behind him, "but why don't you smell?"

"What?" said Ned, startled. "Why should I smell?"

"I asked a question first," replied the voice, "and you can't answer a question with a question. It's rude. But then you're a gnome, so I suppose rudeness is all that can be expected from you … so why don't you smell then?" Ned turned to see a rabbit peeking its head out of a burrow behind him.

"Well, that's the problem," said Ned. "Not that it's any of your business, but I don't like dirt and mud and I hate being rude to people."

"I see," scoffed the rabbit. "A clean, polite gnome. I suppose you expect me to believe that, do you? All gnomes are rude, dirty and smell horrible." The rabbit sniffed loudly. "I don't like gnomes, never have and never shall."

"Oh," said the gnome. "Well, what makes you think rabbits are so perfect, always digging holes for us little folk to fall down?" and so saying, he turned his back on the rabbit.

"Do you really like being clean?" ventured the rabbit, after a while. "Doesn't that make life a bit difficult with the other gnomes?"

"Of course it does," replied Ned. "I've been trying all morning to like mud and enjoy the smell. Yesterday I even practiced being rude, but it's no good," he sighed. "All the other gnomes laugh at me, you know."

The gnome and the rabbit sat for a while side by side, deep in thought.

"Got it," said the rabbit suddenly. "I think I know where there might be some clean gnomes, although I've only seen them from a distance," she admitted, "so I don't know about the politeness bit."

"Really? Where? Please tell me." The gnome jumped up.

"I'll do better than that, I'll show you. Follow me!" And the rabbit hopped off with Ned following closely behind.

Soon they arrived at the top of a steep hill. Climbing down, they came to a house, the sort that humans live in. Surrounding the house was a garden and in the garden was a large pond. Sitting round the pond were several very clean gnomes.

"Ooh, look at them," said Ned in awe. He left the rabbit nibbling plants and flowers in the garden and went to talk to the gnomes.

"Hello, I'm Ned," he said to a gnome who was sitting holding a tiny fishing rod.

"Sshh," hissed the gnome. "We don't talk during the day, we only talk at night." And with that he sat staring ahead, refusing to say another word.

Going back to the rabbit, Ned explained: "They only talk at night, so I think I'll wait and talk to them then."

"Right-oh," said the rabbit, who had taken quite a liking to Ned. "I'll pop back later and see how you're getting on."

Ned found a large bush near the pond. He wriggled into the centre of it, made himself comfortable and fell asleep.

Later, when the stars were out, Ned woke up. Remembering where he was, he crawled excitedly out of the bush and went up to the gnome he'd spoken to earlier.

"Hello," he said. "My name is Ned."

"Sshh," whispered the gnome, "you'll frighten the fish."

"Can I whisper to you?" whispered Ned.

"If you must," replied the gnome.

In hushed tones Ned explained his problem and said that if they were all nice, clean, polite gnomes, then he would like to join them please. The gnome thought for a while. "O.K.," he said eventually. "My name's Grunt. Go and sit over there," and he pointed to a space between two other gnomes.

Ned did as he was told.

"Hello," said Ned to the gnome on his left. "My name is Ned. What's yours?"

"Sshh," said the gnome. "We aren't allowed to talk much in case we disturb the fish, or worse still, wake up the humans."

Ned sat quietly for a while, then, feeling stiff, he got up to stretch his legs.

"Sit still," hissed a voice to his right. "We aren't allowed to move, we might…"

"Disturb the fish," finished Ned. "Yes, I thought as much. Don't you get bored?"

"Of course we don't," whispered the gnome. "We've trained ourselves not to."

Later, the wind started to blow and one of the gnomes fell over, but no one went to help him.

"Why doesn't he get up? Is he hurt?" Ned asked the gnome next to him, in surprise.

"No," came the reply. "He's made of plastic, as are some of the others. They belong to the humans."

Ned looked round and thought to himself, "I can't tell the difference."

"Do you live like this all the time?" he asked the gnome to his right.

"Of course. It is our job to watch over the fish. We have to protect them."

Ned sat for a while longer. At the far end of the garden he could see that his friend the rabbit had returned. Quietly he left the pond and went over to her.

"I have never been so bored in all my life," he told the rabbit. "My friends might be rude and dirty, and they might smell a bit, but at least they're not boring."

"Time to go home, I think," said the rabbit.

When Ned finally arrived home, everybody made a huge fuss of him. He'd been greatly missed. He told the other gnomes about his adventures and they were all very upset that he had nearly left them and so it was decided that they should make a pact.

It was agreed that no gnome would mind if Ned was clean, sweet smelling and polite, as long as Ned did not mind that the others were sometimes rude, almost always dirty, or that they smelled a bit. After that Ned was never ever tempted to leave his gnome home again, although he did sometimes go for long walks with his special friend the rabbit.

A MONSTER HIT!

WRITTEN BY CANDY WALLACE

It was a Tuesday when Kevin discovered there was a monster living in the television. He had just settled down to watch his favourite cartoon programme with a ginormous glass of lemonade and a jumbo packet of crisps. Reggie the cat had been sleeping peacefully on the rug, ears and whiskers twitching as he dreamed happily of a wrestling match with a giant mouse, where, as usual, the score was Reggie 1, Mouse 0. Everything normal then, in Kevin's house.

Kevin took a huge mouthful of crisps and a big gulp of lemonade and settled down to watch *The Adventures of Fancy Frog*, a gripping tale of a gentleman frog who wore a spotted bow tie and carried a walking cane.

This week, he was doing battle with Nasty Newt the pond gangster. It had just got to the bit where Fancy Frog was about to rescue a rather pretty goldfish in distress when a big hairy hand reached out of the back of the television and grabbed Kevin's packet of crisps. The packet disappeared back into the television and Kevin couldn't hear what Fancy Frog was saying for the noise of crunching crisps

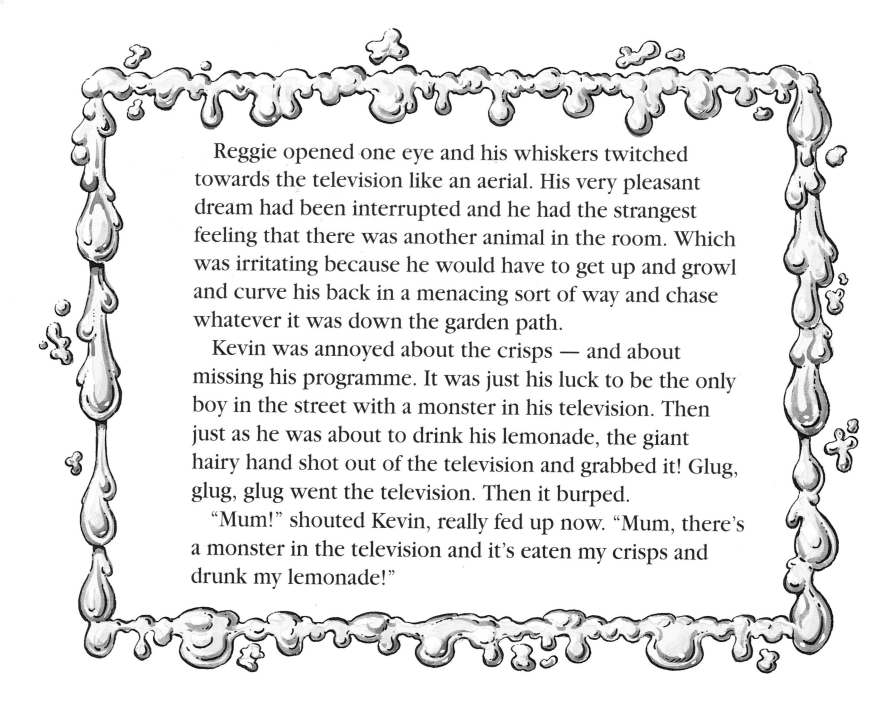

Reggie opened one eye and his whiskers twitched towards the television like an aerial. His very pleasant dream had been interrupted and he had the strangest feeling that there was another animal in the room. Which was irritating because he would have to get up and growl and curve his back in a menacing sort of way and chase whatever it was down the garden path.

Kevin was annoyed about the crisps — and about missing his programme. It was just his luck to be the only boy in the street with a monster in his television. Then just as he was about to drink his lemonade, the giant hairy hand shot out of the television and grabbed it! Glug, glug, glug went the television. Then it burped.

"Mum!" shouted Kevin, really fed up now. "Mum, there's a monster in the television and it's eaten my crisps and drunk my lemonade!"

"Yes, dear," called Mum from the other room. "Your dad will fix it for you in a minute."

Kevin sighed. Dad had been trying all day to build some shelves in the garage. Every time he put them up they fell down again. Last time Kevin had seen Dad he had a purple face and was jumping up and down on a pile of wooden planks. Not the best time to ask Dad to get rid of a monster in the television. There wasn't likely to be a chapter on it in his DIY book either.

He decided to call his friend Eric.

"Hello, Eric, it's Kevin here. Yes, I know Fancy Frog's on the telly at the moment, sorry. But I've got a monster in my television. Can you come round and give me a hand?"

When Kevin got back to the living room, Reggie was sitting on the top of the television with his head right down and his nose to the screen, mesmerised.

Fancy Frog had disappeared from the screen and instead there was a huge, horrible, hairy monster face, grinning and chuckling and poking its tongue out at Reggie. Reggie's fur was standing on end and he kept swiping at the face with his paw, but the monster was safely inside the screen.

Then Grandma came in.

"Is the weather on yet, dear?" she asked Kevin.

"No, sorry Grandma," he answered. "I'm afraid we've got a monster in our television."

"But I always watch the weather!" said Grandma. "Can't you just change the channel?"

They tried, but the hairy monster was on every channel! Grandma decided she'd go next door and watch the weather on their television instead.

"Whatever is the world coming to?" she muttered.

The big hairy hand emerged from the television again and grabbed Reggie's tail. Before Kevin could stop him, the monster was swinging poor Reggie around before hurling him onto the sofa, where he landed in a crumpled heap. The face on the TV screen croaked with glee. Reggie wasn't amused. He picked himself up, put his tail in the air, and with a disdainful sniff over his shoulder, stalked out of the room.

Just then, Eric arrived.

"Have you tried unplugging him?" he suggested helpfully. Kevin hadn't, so they tried. But the big hairy hand just shot out and plugged it in again. It was a real nuisance.

The neighbours came over with Grandma to have a look at the monster. Mr and Mrs Johnson had several suggestions, from making a citizen's arrest to calling the fire brigade. But Kevin's mum thought they might spray water all over her nice new living room carpet.

The word soon spread that there was a monster in the television at number 28. Before long there was a queue outside and Kevin and Eric were organising refreshments and doing a roaring trade in cups of tea and Mum's homemade scones. Dad didn't know what was going on. He was still trying to put up shelves in the garage, but Mum helped Kevin put up a barrier with string around the television. This was after the monster grabbed Mrs Taylor's new hat and ate it in front of her on the screen, giggling as he did so. He even let out a big burp when he'd finished! Mrs Taylor was not impressed.

Two hours later a large van drew up outside and several people got out carrying cameras and microphones.

"Hello!" they shouted, as they marched through the front door, past the waiting neighbours and visitors.

"We're from TVB News. We've come to interview Kevin about the TV monster!"

"How long has this monster been in your television?" asked the lady reporter in a concerned voice. "Will this change your life? How do you feel?"

"Well, he's been here since Fancy Frog started about a quarter past five," replied Kevin. "We feel really fed up because that's our favourite programme and it will change our life because we'll have to go next door to watch it."

The lady reporter nodded in a caring sort of way.

"Thank you, Kevin. This is Anna Badger-Jones at 28 Acacia Avenue, reporting for TVB."

The next morning, Kevin was invited onto breakfast television to talk about his monster. The TV company came and picked up Kevin and his television with the monster inside. In the studio they plugged the monster

in and asked him questions about the world situation. All he did was cackle and croak and try and grab the cameras with his big hairy hand, but he was a big hit with the viewers. TVB offered Kevin a brand new television in return for leaving his old television with them. They wanted to give the monster his own regular spot on the breakfast show.

So after that Kevin and Eric were able to watch Fancy Frog every week and enjoy their crisps and lemonade in peace. Now and then, they would turn on the TV before school and catch *The Mega Monster Show* where the monster had guests like pop stars and government ministers. Even Reggie would sit on the rug and watch, with an occasional twitch of his whiskers.

It was nice to see the monster now and again, but even nicer to be able to turn him off!

WASH DAY BLUES

WRITTEN BY CLAIRE STEEDEN

Wishy Washy the fairy lived and worked in fairyland. He owned a shop called Wishy's Washeteria which had a little flat above. He spent each day hand washing fairy wings, which was a very important job as you can imagine. Fairy wings are very expensive and Wishy took great pride in his job.

He was always very busy and today was no exception. At the weekend there was to be a huge party where the fairy council would announce which lucky fairies would

sit on top of the Christmas trees in people's homes at Christmas time. All day long fairies were coming in with sets of wings and asking if they would be ready by Saturday, as they wanted to look their best.

"Oh, I'll never wash all these wings in time," Wishy said to himself. "Each pair takes so long to do. It's Thursday afternoon already."

Wishy lifted a pair of wings gently into the tub, filled with warm water. He picked up a packet of Fairiel washing powder to sprinkle over the wings, but realized that it was empty.

"Oh, bother. That's all I need. Now what am I going to do. I've got a whole pile of wings to wash and no powder. I'll never have it all done by Saturday.

Wishy remembered seeing an advertisement in the newspaper for washing machines. "Maybe it's time I bought one," he thought. He found the paper and read the advertisement aloud.

"No more wash-day blues. Put a whizz into your wash with a brand new washing machine and let it work while you play!"

"Perfect. That's just what I need." Wishy phoned the company and they sent a fairy round to install one right away.

"Just read the instruction booklet and it will tell you how it works," said the plumber fairy, handing him a big box of powder.

"Thank you. I'll soon get all this washing done now," said Wishy.

After saying goodbye he went to look at his new machine. It was very big and covered in buttons and flashing lights. Wishy sat down and started to read the instructions, but they were far too complicated.

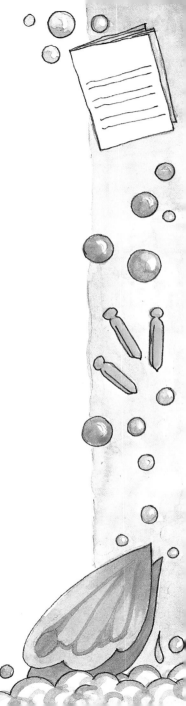

"It'll take me ages to work all of this out. If I just put it on a simple program it should be okay," Wishy said to himself. "Besides, I've got an important evening ahead and I must go and get ready. It's the final of the fairyland quiz competition tonight. If I win I can spend the money on a holiday. I haven't had one for years."

Wishy took all the wings off their hangers, loaded them into the machine, put in some of the new powder and set the machine on what he thought was a low setting. Then off he flew to the quiz, hoping to win the star prize so he could travel to the mountains.

Wishy took his seat just as the contest began. The host asked the contestants lots of questions, and to his surprise, Wishy ended up in the final three, with one tie-breaker question to answer:

"What," asked the fairy host, "is the highest mountain in Fairyland?"

"Mount Sparkle," answered Wishy.

"Correct. You've won the competition and a thousand fairy pieces!"

Everyone cheered, especially Wishy. He could have a holiday at last! He could not believe his luck. A lovely new washing machine and winning the competition all in one day! And to think he had been so miserable this morning.

Arriving home, he took off his wings and was just climbing into bed when he heard an awful rumbling noise coming from downstairs. Pulling on his dressing gown, Wishy went to investigate. The noise seemed to be coming from the laundry. Nervously, he stepped into the dark room.

"Yuk! What's that?" Wishy's feet were covered in something cold and tickly. He turned on the light and looked around. He couldn't believe his eyes. The whole floor was covered in soap suds, which were pouring out of his new machine. He ran to turn it off.

"Oh my goodness! What a mess. I hope the wings are all right," he said, opening the machine's door.

First of all he pulled out a pair that were enormous. "Oh, no. They've stretched. This pair are ruined. Oh dear!"

He reached in and pulled out another pair which looked the right size, but when he held them up they were full of holes. "Oh dear. They're all torn. I won't be able to mend holes that size," he sighed.

Suds were still oozing out onto the floor as he reached in and pulled out a bundle of wings. As he untangled them he let out a groan. "Ooh, all the colours have run. The new automatic powder I used can't have been right for these wings. The colours have mixed and made the wings patchy. What a disaster!" he cried.

Tears welled up in Wishy's eyes as he pulled out the last pair of wings. They were tiny.

"Oh dear. The water must have got too hot. It's shrunk this pair."

Wishy sat on his little wooden stool and cried, but his tears were lost amongst the bubbles. "All the wings are ruined and the fairies need them for Saturday. What am I going to do?" he wept.

Wishy spent all night clearing up the soapy mess.

"This will teach me not to be impatient. If I'd washed them by hand I wouldn't be in this mess," he said to himself. "I can't repair the wings, so I'll have to give each customer the money to buy a new pair. I'll have to use the money I won in the competition last night."

Wishy spent all the next day explaining to his customers about the machine and their ruined wings. After handing out money all day he only had twenty fairy pieces left of his prize money.

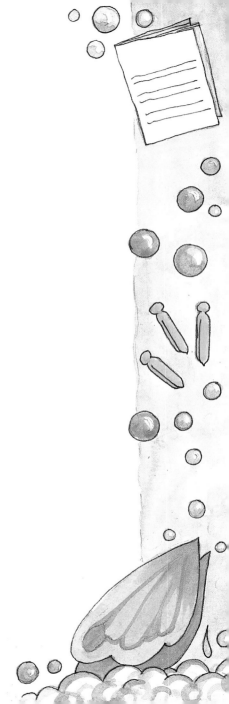

"At least everyone will have lovely new wings for tomorrow night. I can always go on holiday next year," sighed Wishy.

On Saturday morning the plumber fairy came to take the washing machine away again. Wishy decided he would always do his washing by hand in future.

That night all the fairies gathered at the grand hall to find out who would be chosen to decorate the Christmas trees. Everyone looked magnificent in their sparkly outfits and shiny new wings.

At eight o'clock a list of names was announced and there was much celebrating amongst the fairies. Just as Wishy was about to leave he heard his name being called out, and he turned to face the fairy speaker.

"Wishy, I understand that it is thanks to you that the fairies all have such beautiful new wings this evening," she said.

I hear you had an accident with your new washing machine, and you spent all the prize money you won in the quiz competition buying new wings for everybody. A thousand fairy pieces is a lot of money. I understand you wanted to spend it on a holiday in the mountains," said the fairy.

"Yes, that's right," replied Wishy.

"Well, you have proved what a hard working, kind and honest fairy you are. Your behaviour deserves some kind of reward." The fairy speaker handed Wishy an envelope.

"Here's some money that your friends and customers have collected for you. Everyone thinks you deserve a holiday, so you will make it to the mountains after all! Enjoy your trip."

Wishy thanked everybody, and when he got home he thought how lucky he was to have his little shop, such caring friends and a lovely holiday to look forward to.

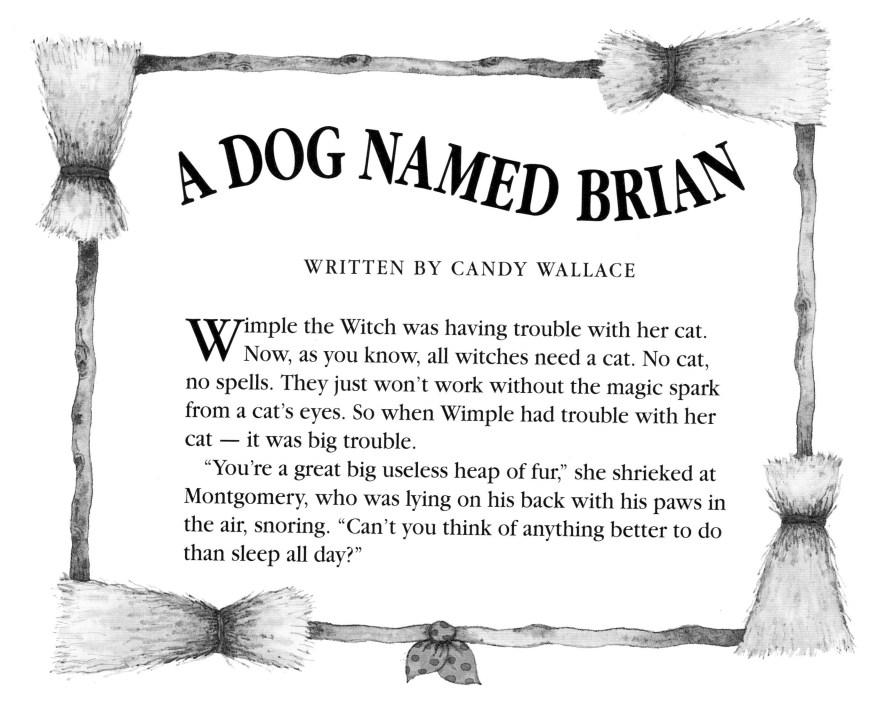

A DOG NAMED BRIAN

WRITTEN BY CANDY WALLACE

Wimple the Witch was having trouble with her cat. Now, as you know, all witches need a cat. No cat, no spells. They just won't work without the magic spark from a cat's eyes. So when Wimple had trouble with her cat — it was big trouble.

"You're a great big useless heap of fur," she shrieked at Montgomery, who was lying on his back with his paws in the air, snoring. "Can't you think of anything better to do than sleep all day?"

Wimple drew back her large foot and booted
him across the room — no mean feat since
Montgomery weighed nearly as much as
a sack of coal. Montgomery rotated in
mid-air twice and came to rest on
his paws with a faint look
of surprise.

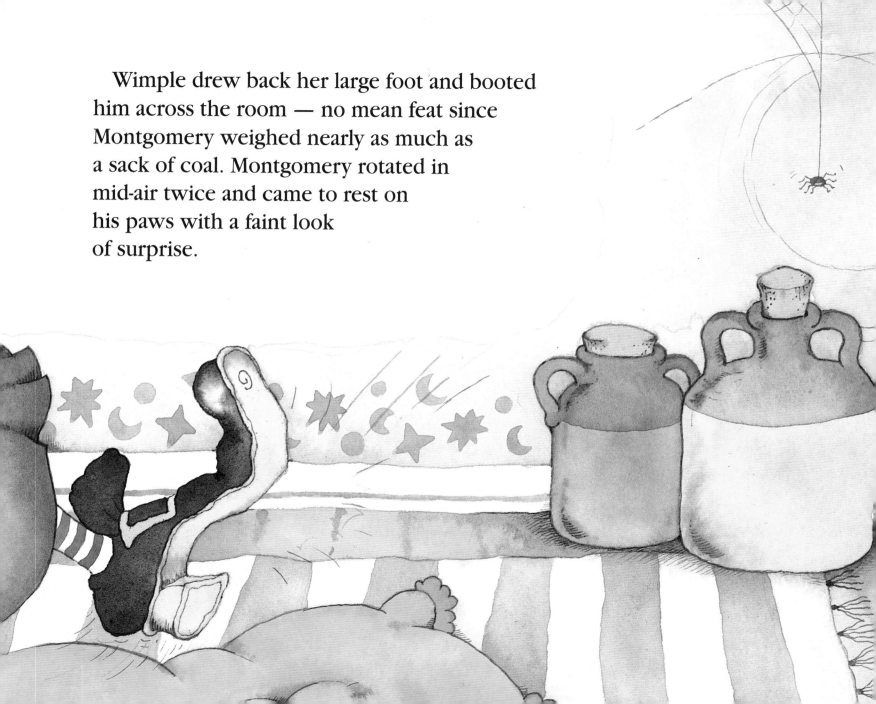

His feelings were more hurt than anything. True, he had slowed down a trifle lately, but frankly, he was getting on a bit now. He'd used up eight-and-a-half lives and all he wanted was a bit of peace.

Wimple put her hands on her hips and glowered at Montgomery, who had keeled over on the spot and fallen into an instant slumber.

"Right!" she screamed. "That's it!" It was time to get another cat. One she could rely on. In two shakes of a rat's tail she was astride her broomstick and on her way to the *Paws for Thought* cat agency.

"I want a sleek, hardworking black cat with a flash of genius. Experience in turning princes into frogs and vice versa would be preferred," she said, to the bored-looking witch behind the counter.

"No," the assistant said.

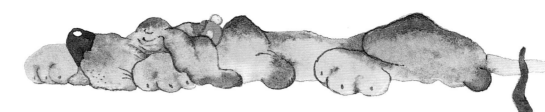

"What do you mean — no?" said Wimple.

"No cats left on our books. We've had a run on them this week."

Wimple turned purple.

"All we've got left is a dog called Brian." While Wimple stood there, speechless, the assistant went into a back room and came back with a huge bloodhound who looked rather depressed. He knew just what would happen. They always took one look at him and shrieked with laughter.

He'd spent three years learning to be a Witch's Personal Assistant and now nobody would hire him.

"I'll take him!" said Wimple suddenly. She was a desperate witch. "I just wish he wasn't quite so big."

The first problem was that there was no way Brian was going to ride on the broomstick. When he got on it it just

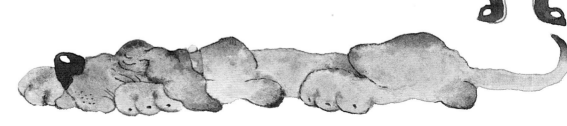

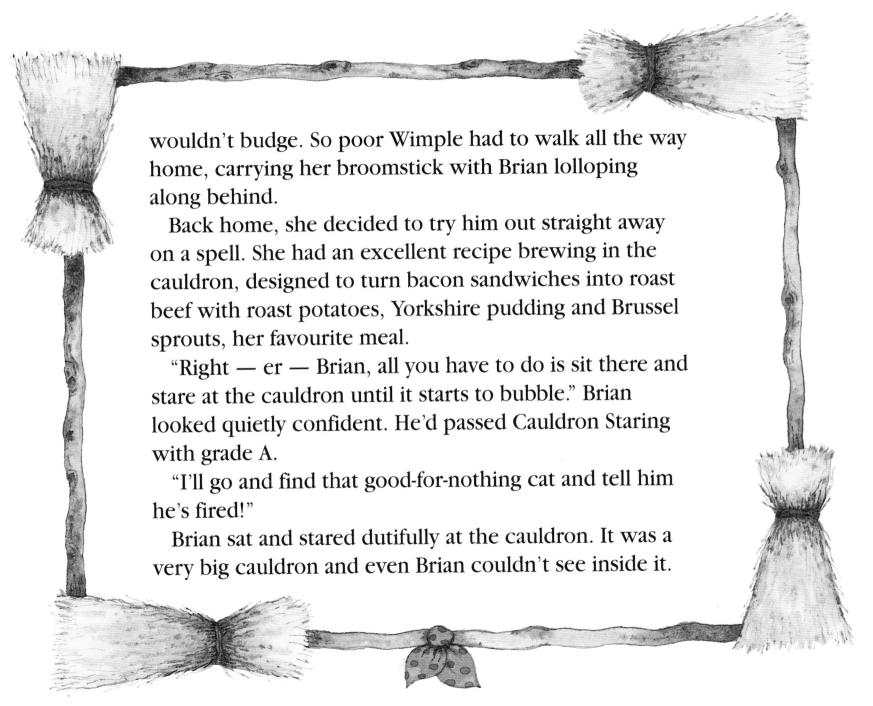

wouldn't budge. So poor Wimple had to walk all the way home, carrying her broomstick with Brian lolloping along behind.

Back home, she decided to try him out straight away on a spell. She had an excellent recipe brewing in the cauldron, designed to turn bacon sandwiches into roast beef with roast potatoes, Yorkshire pudding and Brussel sprouts, her favourite meal.

"Right — er — Brian, all you have to do is sit there and stare at the cauldron until it starts to bubble." Brian looked quietly confident. He'd passed Cauldron Staring with grade A.

"I'll go and find that good-for-nothing cat and tell him he's fired!"

Brian sat and stared dutifully at the cauldron. It was a very big cauldron and even Brian couldn't see inside it.

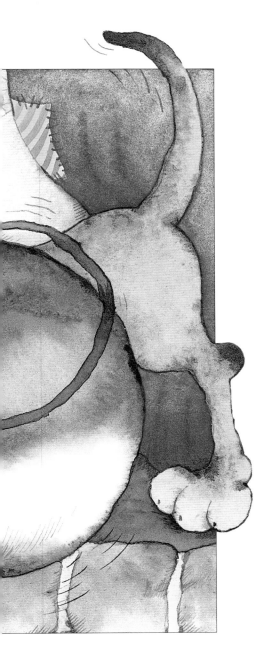

So he didn't know whether it was bubbling or not. He thought he'd better check and put his paws up on the top of the cauldron to look in. The big pot swayed and tilted and crash! It toppled over. All the bubbling liquid flowed onto the floor — and over Montgomery who was busy escaping from Wimple. Montgomery felt very strange for a minute and then turned into a Brussel sprout. Wimple, following behind, stopped dead in her tracks.

"You stupid dog! Quick, we'll have to mix another spell. She thumbed through her recipe book until she found Brussel Sprout — Into Cat, page 62. "We need some toadstools. Go and get some this minute!" Poor Brian was feeling very embarrassed and loped off into the garden, determined he would prove himself this time.
He came back carrying a basket full of toadstools.

Strangely enough, Wimple didn't seem pleased. She was staring out of the window with eyes like saucers, clenching her fists.

"You've — just — trampled — all — over — my — magic — herbs," she said, very slowly. "The ones that have taken me a year to grow…" Brian thought that now would be a good time to disappear for a while.

When Wimple had calmed down, she mixed the spell, muttering to herself about stupid dogs and cats, and managed to restore Montgomery to his previous furry self, none the worse for wear. But then she dropped her recipe book into the cauldron and it disintegrated in a puff of smoke.

That was the last straw. Wimple was literally hopping mad. She jumped up and down and stamped her feet, hopping all over the room. Then bump! Her head hit the shelf where she kept all her secret jars and bottles. A big dusty jar marked Frog Mixture teetered on the brink, then fell over, the thick green liquid pouring down onto Wimple's head.

When Brian and Montgomery crept in a little later, Wimple didn't seem to be there. There was just this small, rather bewildered frog sitting on the floor.

Brian looked up at the shelf where all the bottles were higgledy piggledy and saw the upturned jar. He looked at Montgomery and Montgomery looked at him. Then they both looked at the frog.

They ran over to where Wimple's recipe book was kept, but there was no sign of it anywhere! Brian and Montgomery would just have to try and remember the right spell between them. Montgomery rushed out into the garden and nibbled off some squashed herbs. Brian took down the jar marked Pickled Slugs and another that said All Purpose Slime — Top Quality. They mixed all the ingredients together in a spare pot and stirred it with their paws. The frog looked on and blinked silently. Together, the cat and dog sat and

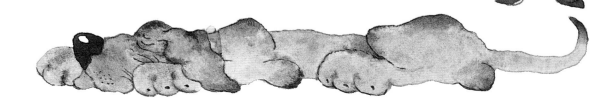

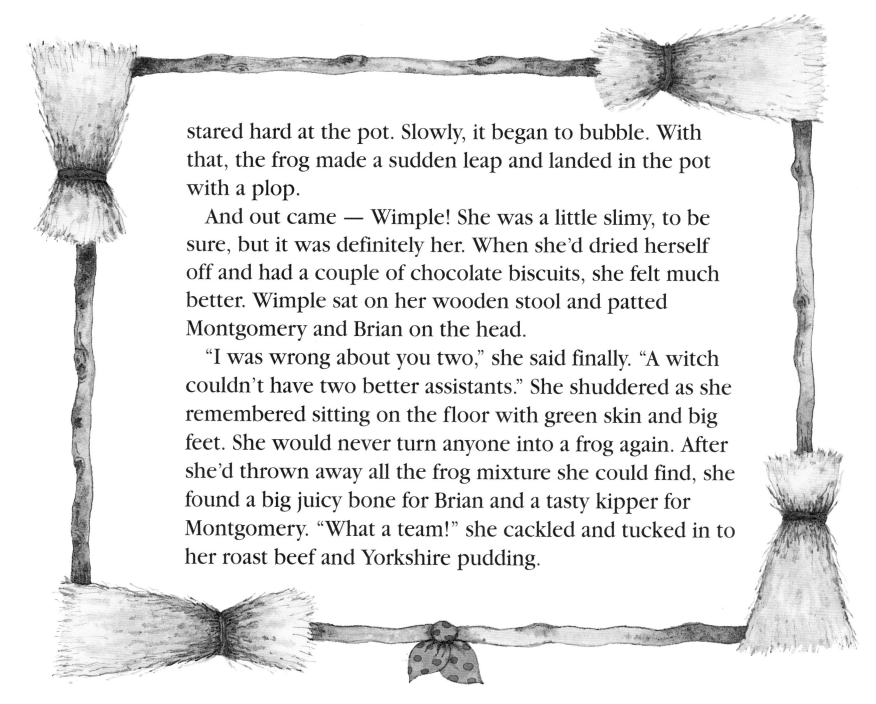

stared hard at the pot. Slowly, it began to bubble. With that, the frog made a sudden leap and landed in the pot with a plop.

And out came — Wimple! She was a little slimy, to be sure, but it was definitely her. When she'd dried herself off and had a couple of chocolate biscuits, she felt much better. Wimple sat on her wooden stool and patted Montgomery and Brian on the head.

"I was wrong about you two," she said finally. "A witch couldn't have two better assistants." She shuddered as she remembered sitting on the floor with green skin and big feet. She would never turn anyone into a frog again. After she'd thrown away all the frog mixture she could find, she found a big juicy bone for Brian and a tasty kipper for Montgomery. "What a team!" she cackled and tucked in to her roast beef and Yorkshire pudding.

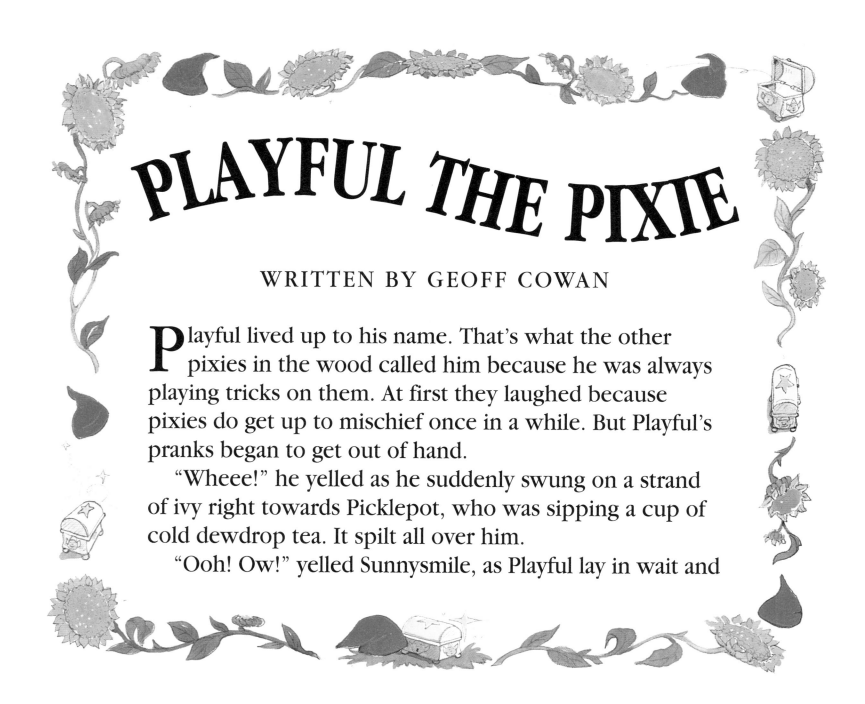

PLAYFUL THE PIXIE

WRITTEN BY GEOFF COWAN

Playful lived up to his name. That's what the other pixies in the wood called him because he was always playing tricks on them. At first they laughed because pixies do get up to mischief once in a while. But Playful's pranks began to get out of hand.

"Wheee!" he yelled as he suddenly swung on a strand of ivy right towards Picklepot, who was sipping a cup of cold dewdrop tea. It spilt all over him.

"Ooh! Ow!" yelled Sunnysmile, as Playful lay in wait and

pelted him with berries. The juice stained Sunnysmile's clothes.

"Grrrgh!" spluttered an unsuspecting Curlytoes when he pulled on his hat and found Playful had filled it with water. Truth was, the pixies were more than a little tired of Playful's non-stop naughtiness. Time and again they asked him to behave.

"A joke's a joke but you've gone too far, Playful," they warned.

"Or not far enough!" grumbled some. "Keep this up and you can go and play in someone else's patch of wood!"

Which is exactly what Playful did. One morning, he climbed out of bed extra early and set off across the meadow into another wood where a band of elves lived. And what a dance he led them, too. Playful made sure he kept himself hidden and puffed pollen on the elves to make them sneeze. While they slept, he swapped their boots around so they didn't fit!

"This is better fun than before," giggled Playful. "Now no one even knows it's me!"

That was until the elves caught him, for elves are much more clever than you might think. They knew someone had to be behind all the odd goings-on, so they laid a trap.

Playful fell for it; or it fell for Playful, to be exact. A carefully placed bag of honey dropped on his hat, bursting open, the next time he tried to creep up on the elves.

"Caught you!" they cried, feeling extremely pleased with themselves as they danced around a very gooey Playful.

"Mess with us and you'll come unstuck!" warned an elf named Echo. He was called Echo because he liked the sound of his own voice.

"I'm in a mess and all stuck up!" cried Playful, miserably.

"Serves you right!" sang Echo. "When you're washed and clean, we'll take you back where you came from."

One of the elves had guessed Playful was from The Other Wood because he'd heard it was full of pixies. When both bands came face to face, the pixies were startled to see Playful with the elves. They weren't so surprised to hear about all the bother he'd caused.

"The least we can do is invite you to a Pixie Party," Picklepot told the elves. "There'll be music, dancing and all the pixie pizzas you can eat!"

And more of Playful's pranks. The fact was he just couldn't seem to help himself. He sprinkled mud on the mushroom seats to make folk sit down with a squelch! He put jelly in a flower-trumpet so wobbly bits were blown out everywhere when the pixie band played; and that was only the start. The elves and pixies were fed up before they'd even eaten anything! When they did sit down to eat they were furious to discover that someone had mixed up all the food and put mustard in the jam sandwiches and tomato ketchup in the sponge cake. Things had gone beyond a joke!

It called for quick thinking before tempers flared. Picklepot and Echo drew up a plan. The first part was easy. For the rest of the party, the elves and pixies would take it in turns to watch Playful very carefully. If he showed the slightest sign of mischief, they would step in and stop him. The second part was harder…

Next morning, when Playful woke, what do you think his first thought of the day was? Which new tricks he should try out, of course! But he never got the chance to play any tricks, because he realised with a terrible shock that he had no idea where he was. And even worse, he was all alone. He was in a part of the wood he had never been to before.

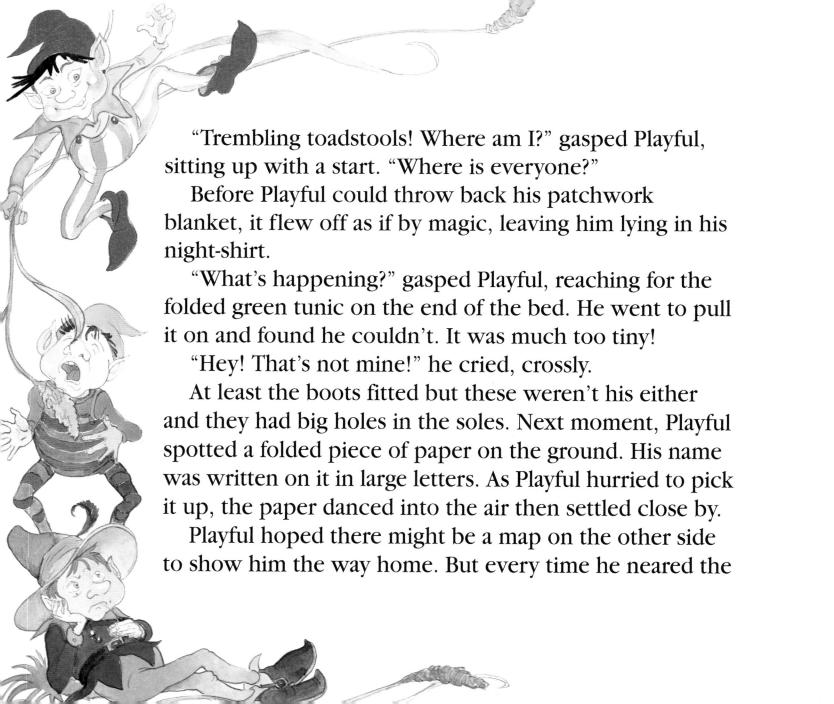

"Trembling toadstools! Where am I?" gasped Playful, sitting up with a start. "Where is everyone?"

Before Playful could throw back his patchwork blanket, it flew off as if by magic, leaving him lying in his night-shirt.

"What's happening?" gasped Playful, reaching for the folded green tunic on the end of the bed. He went to pull it on and found he couldn't. It was much too tiny!

"Hey! That's not mine!" he cried, crossly.

At least the boots fitted but these weren't his either and they had big holes in the soles. Next moment, Playful spotted a folded piece of paper on the ground. His name was written on it in large letters. As Playful hurried to pick it up, the paper danced into the air then settled close by.

Playful hoped there might be a map on the other side to show him the way home. But every time he neared the paper, it fluttered further away until it landed long enough for Playful to pounce. Whoosh! A net hidden under some leaves sprang up and closed around him. Playful was whisked off his feet and found himself dangling in mid-air.

"Caught you!" cried a voice as Playful struggled.

"Let me down, whoever you are! Please stop playing tricks on me!" he called, dizzily. He was really rather frightened indeed.

"Only if you stop playing them on all of us!" said Picklepot, who stepped out from behind a tree with the other pixies.

"And us! And us!" repeated Echo who appeared with the elves.

"Yes! I promise!" said Playful, who was relieved to see them. They gently lowered the net and helped him out.

Now Playful noticed Sunnysmile holding the bed blanket tied to a long thread that he had used to pull it away. Another was tied to the note Playful had chased to lure him to the net. Curlytoes happily handed over Playful's proper clothes.

"We carried your bed here while you slept," grinned Picklepot. "Then we set up the other tricks."

"They're not funny when someone plays them on you, are they?" said Echo sternly.

"I hadn't thought of that," agreed Playful, shaking his head. "It isn't very nice, is it? I promise that from today I won't play any more tricks on anyone. Except maybe just a small one on Sundays."

The elves and the pixies all chuckled, and Picklepot said that was good enough for him. The elves agreed and returned to their own wood. From that day on, Playful was the best-behaved pixie you could imagine — except on Sundays, when everyone wondered who's turn it would be for him to play tricks on! The pixies even gave him a new name 'Goodasgold', and he became a very helpful little pixie indeed.

So if you ever chance to meet a very polite pixie, remember who it could be and be careful never to ask him, "How's tricks?!"

Especially on a Sunday!

DESMOND THE DRAGON

WRITTEN BY AMBER HUNT

Young Desmond the Dragon was by now absolutely, utterly, and almost nearly sure that he wasn't a dragon. Oh, he was a respectable size, and growing all the time, and he was covered from ears to tail with very tough and very green scales. He had a forked tongue, just like all his friends, and four sets of fine claws as well as a good loud dragon-type roar. Desmond had to admit that he did look a lot like his mum and dad, but, despite all this, Desmond was still worried that he might not be a real dragon.

Each morning he looked in the mirror, twisting around to examine his back and each morning he saw — nothing. Dragons had wings, didn't they? If he was a dragon, where were his wings?

Then, after he had looked in the mirror, Desmond
would go outside the cave into the garden and breathe
out hard. Nothing. Dragons breathed fire, didn't they? If
he was a dragon, where was his fire?

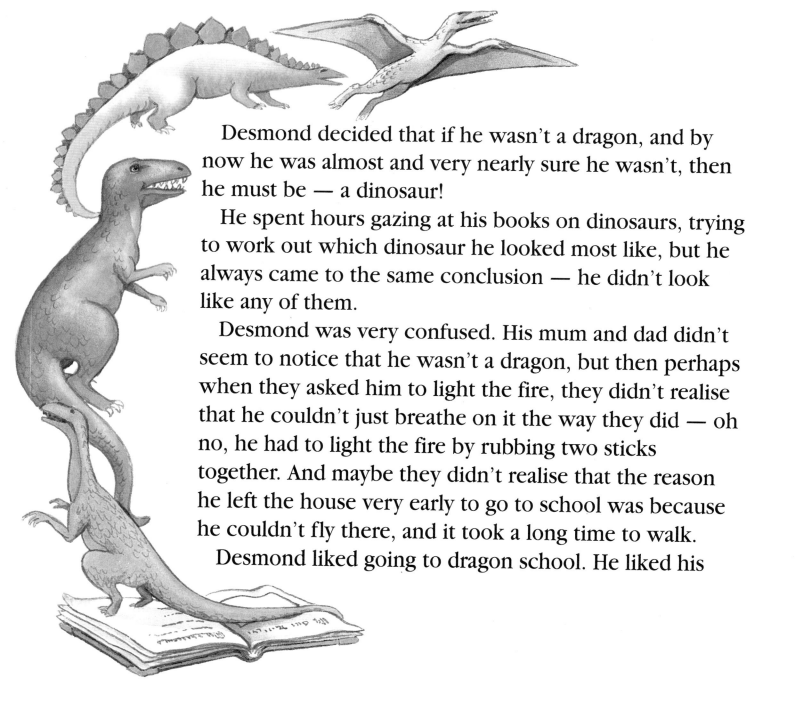

Desmond decided that if he wasn't a dragon, and by now he was almost and very nearly sure he wasn't, then he must be — a dinosaur!

He spent hours gazing at his books on dinosaurs, trying to work out which dinosaur he looked most like, but he always came to the same conclusion — he didn't look like any of them.

Desmond was very confused. His mum and dad didn't seem to notice that he wasn't a dragon, but then perhaps when they asked him to light the fire, they didn't realise that he couldn't just breathe on it the way they did — oh no, he had to light the fire by rubbing two sticks together. And maybe they didn't realise that the reason he left the house very early to go to school was because he couldn't fly there, and it took a long time to walk.

Desmond liked going to dragon school. He liked his

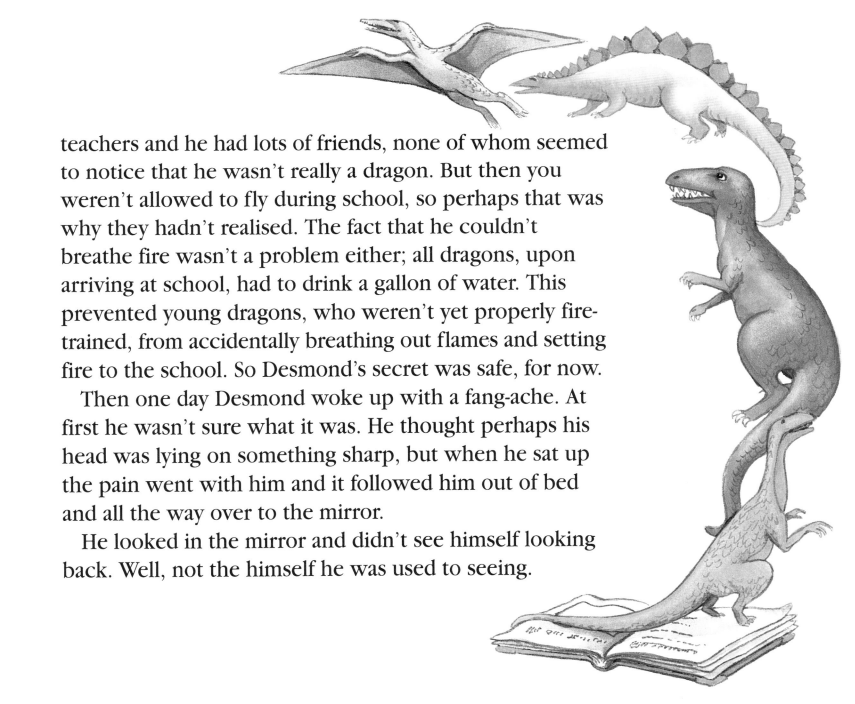

teachers and he had lots of friends, none of whom seemed to notice that he wasn't really a dragon. But then you weren't allowed to fly during school, so perhaps that was why they hadn't realised. The fact that he couldn't breathe fire wasn't a problem either; all dragons, upon arriving at school, had to drink a gallon of water. This prevented young dragons, who weren't yet properly fire-trained, from accidentally breathing out flames and setting fire to the school. So Desmond's secret was safe, for now.

Then one day Desmond woke up with a fang-ache. At first he wasn't sure what it was. He thought perhaps his head was lying on something sharp, but when he sat up the pain went with him and it followed him out of bed and all the way over to the mirror.

He looked in the mirror and didn't see himself looking back. Well, not the himself he was used to seeing.

The dragon, or possibly not dragon, he was looking at, had a huge swelling on the side of its face.

Desmond rushed downstairs to his mum.

"Mum," he mumbled, "look at my face. It has gone all lumpy and bumpy."

Desmond's mum looked at his face and, trying not to laugh, said, "Oh dear, I think you have been eating too many chocolate-covered bones. We'd better go and see Morris the Magician. He's a wonderful fangtist, amongst other things." She winked at Desmond's dad, and while Desmond went to get his hat, said to him, "I think it's time to get a couple of other things sorted out too while we're there, don't you, dear?"

So off they went to see Morris. "It's such a nice day," said Mrs Dragon, with a knowing smile. "I think we'll walk." And they did, much to Desmond's relief.

Desmond sat in Morris the Magician's special chair and waited, while his mum talked to Morris outside. He was trying to be brave and fearless, as he knew a good dragon should be, but his knees kept knocking together at the thought of what Morris might do. Then Morris came in and sat on a stool next to him and asked Desmond to open his mouth wide.

"This won't hurt," he said.

"Uh, huh, uh, huh, mmm," muttered Morris. "Ah yes, yes, I have it, I can see the problem." He smiled at Desmond. "You have a bone caught behind one of your fangs and it's pressing into the gum. The bone is stuck quite fast which is why your fang brush couldn't get it out. You do brush your fangs, don't you, Desmond?" asked Morris, sternly.

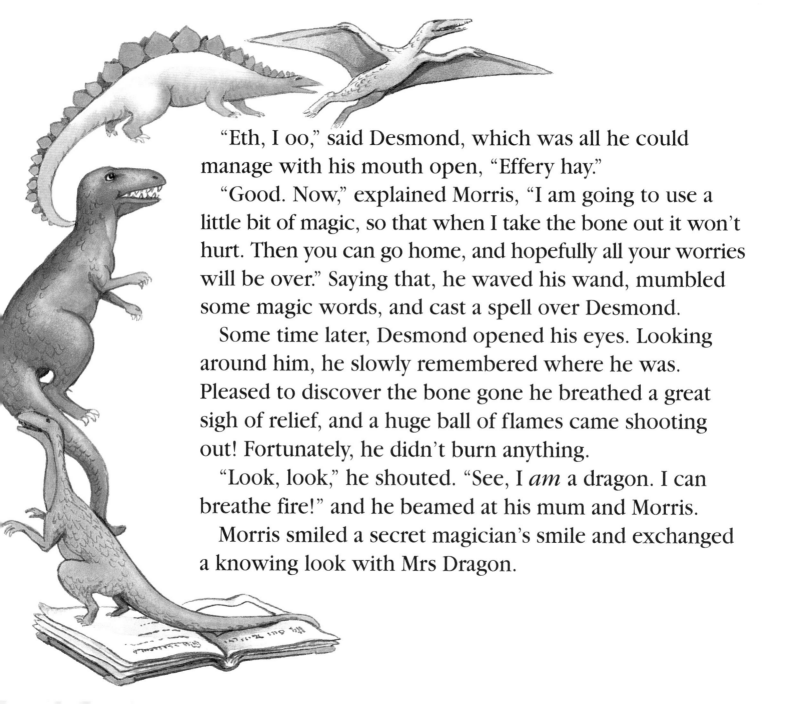

"Eth, I oo," said Desmond, which was all he could manage with his mouth open, "Effery hay."

"Good. Now," explained Morris, "I am going to use a little bit of magic, so that when I take the bone out it won't hurt. Then you can go home, and hopefully all your worries will be over." Saying that, he waved his wand, mumbled some magic words, and cast a spell over Desmond.

Some time later, Desmond opened his eyes. Looking around him, he slowly remembered where he was. Pleased to discover the bone gone he breathed a great sigh of relief, and a huge ball of flames came shooting out! Fortunately, he didn't burn anything.

"Look, look," he shouted. "See, I *am* a dragon. I can breathe fire!" and he beamed at his mum and Morris.

Morris smiled a secret magician's smile and exchanged a knowing look with Mrs Dragon.

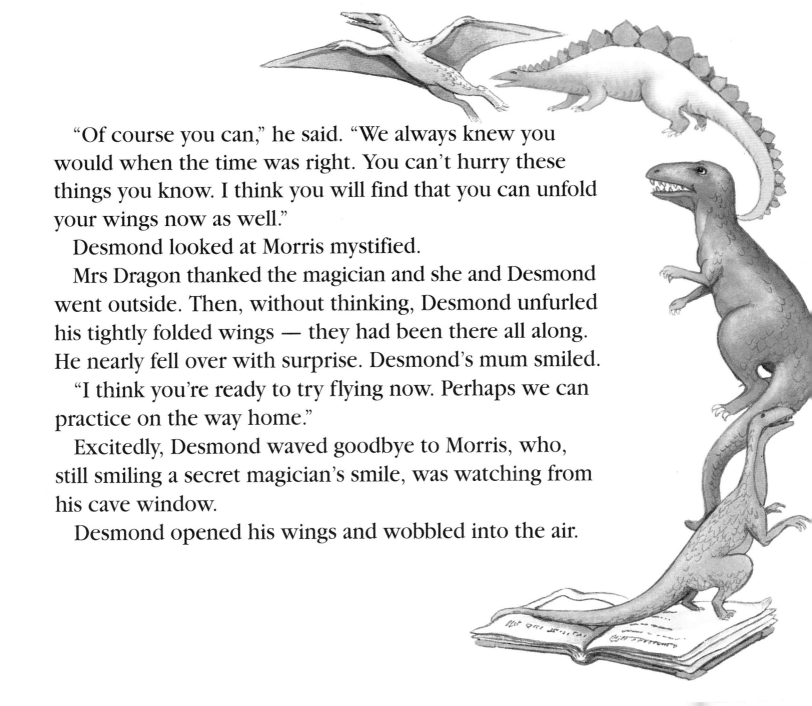

"Of course you can," he said. "We always knew you would when the time was right. You can't hurry these things you know. I think you will find that you can unfold your wings now as well."

Desmond looked at Morris mystified.

Mrs Dragon thanked the magician and she and Desmond went outside. Then, without thinking, Desmond unfurled his tightly folded wings — they had been there all along. He nearly fell over with surprise. Desmond's mum smiled.

"I think you're ready to try flying now. Perhaps we can practice on the way home."

Excitedly, Desmond waved goodbye to Morris, who, still smiling a secret magician's smile, was watching from his cave window.

Desmond opened his wings and wobbled into the air.

Then, his confidence growing, he soared up into the
sky and flew round a few times — looking and feeling
like the noble dragon he was.

And finally, he flew home for tea with his mum.

BIGGER, BIGGEST, BEST

WRITTEN BY DAN ABNETT

Fortyodd was a giant. He was called Fortyodd because he was forty-odd times as tall as a man. His hands were as big as bulldozers and his feet were as big as barges. He was huge. If you spread your arms out wide, it wouldn't be as wide as his smile.

Fortyodd was a gardener. He looked after the Great Forest. He strode through his forest in the way a farmer marches through his cabbage patch, bending over to prune an oak tree here, leaning down to replant a birch tree there.

Fortyodd liked his job. Fortyodd liked the Great Forest. He called it his lawn.

One morning, his friend Fiftytimes came round and knocked on the door of his shed. Fortyodd's shed was nine times as large as an aircraft hangar, so the echo of Fiftytimes' knock rolled round the hills and dales for a week or two.

"Morning, Fiftytimes," rumbled Fortyodd as he came to the door of his shed, a steaming vat of tea in his hand. "The reservoir's just boiling. Do you fancy a vat of tea?"

"Don't mind if I do," replied Fiftytimes.

Fortyodd washed up another vat in his swimming pool-sized sink. He used a small evergreen tree as a brush. "Sugar?" he asked.

"Two barrows, please," replied Fiftytimes, making himself comfortable on the sofa. It wasn't a sofa, actually. It was a small hill that Fortyodd had dragged into the shed and covered with a circus tent, but they called it a sofa.

Fortyodd scooped two wheelbarrows of sugar into Fiftytimes' vat of tea and stirred it with a lamppost.

"So what can I do for you?" Fortyodd asked as they settled down to their vats of tea.

"I thought I had better tell you," said Fiftytimes, "old

Twoscore is planning to enter his prize cabbage in the Harvest Show next week. He's hoping to win the Big Veg prize."

"I didn't know Twoscore had a prize cabbage," said Fortyodd, rather uneasily.

"That's why I thought I'd better tell you," said Fiftytimes. "I was passing his garden just yesterday, and I saw his cabbage patch. It's a handsome crop he's got."

Fortyodd frowned. His brow crinkled so deeply, you could have lost whole flocks of sheep in the wrinkles. You see, every year, his famous pumpkins won the Big Veg rosette at the Harvest Show. There wasn't a giant in the land who grew vegetables that were bigger or better or more beautiful than Fortyodd's pumpkins.

"How are your pumpkins doing this year, anyway?" asked Fiftytimes.

Fortyodd took his friend out into the garden and showed him. There were a dozen splendid pumpkins, each one the size of a hot air balloon.

"Very impressive," said Fiftytimes, "but I have to say, old Twoscore's prize cabbage is bigger than your biggest pumpkin."

Fortyodd was very unhappy. After his friend had gone, he stomped about his garden, grumbling and moaning to himself. The ground shook, and from a mile away it sounded like a serious thunderstorm. Fortyodd tried to do some weeding to take his mind off it, pulling up some chestnut trees, roots and all. But his heart wasn't in it. He went back to his shed and slammed the door behind him.

Fortyodd knew that he had to do something quickly, or Twoscore would win the prize. Fortyodd was very proud of the row of Big Veg rosettes over his fireplace, and couldn't bear the thought that there wouldn't be a new one to pin

up this year. Besides, Big Veg was all he knew. It was his speciality. He hadn't got a particular talent for any of the other prize categories like jam making or tree arranging. Big Veg was his thing. He was a Big Veg giant.

Fortyodd took down the gardening book that his grandfather, old Seventysomething, had compiled. It was chock full of splendid tricks and tips. If nothing else, old Seventysomething had been the tallest gardener of his generation.

Fortyodd laid the book open on his desk. The open book was as wide as the wingspan of a jumbo jet. Fortyodd put on his reading glasses (two telescope lenses from an observatory held in carefully bent scaffolding) and studied the book carefully, slowly turning the rugby pitch-sized pages.

Finally, just as it was getting dark, he found something.

There on page four thousand and one was a recipe for Plant Growth Formula. It seemed his grandfather had got the recipe from a retired witch.

That evening, Fortyodd made up the recipe. It took hours of careful mixing, measuring and stirring. At last, he was sure he had it pretty much right. He poured the formula out of the cement mixer and into a huge pair of furnace bellows. Then, with his lamp in one hand and the bellows in the other, he went out into the dark, to his pumpkin patch nearby. The pumpkins looked huge and golden in the moonlight.

Fortyodd took the bellows and pumped a spray of formula over his prize vegetables. The magic formula twinkled electric green in the darkness. Satisfied with a job well done, Fortyodd admired his handiwork. Already, the pumpkins looked even more huge and golden. Then Fortyodd went off to bed.

Next morning, Fortyodd's alarm (a church clocktower on the bedside table) woke him at eight, and he was surprised to see that it was still dark. He went to the door and tried to open it, but it wouldn't budge. He went to the window, and found he couldn't see anything outside except a wall of bright orange.

Rather worried, Fortyodd took the door off its hinges and found that the doorway was completely blocked by the biggest pumpkin he had ever seen. It was acres across from side to side. Fortyodd squeezed out of the doorway and climbed up onto the top of the enormous vegetable.

High up on top, it was like standing on an orange mountain, and there were several other orange mountains next to it. The huge pumpkins completely surrounded his garden shed, and seemed in danger of crushing it.

The formula had certainly worked.

Fortyodd wasn't really sure what to do next, but he knew that, one way or another, it would involve a lot of pumpkin-eating.

Everyone thereabouts agreed that Fortyodd's pumpkins were the biggest Big Veg they had ever seen. People flocked from miles around to see them. Families of giants had their photographs taken posing in front of the great pumpkin range. Passing dragons looked down at the pumpkins in astonishment. Dwarf mountaineers climbed them and stuck flags in the top.

Twoscore's prize cabbages won the Big Veg rosette at the Harvest Show, of course. Everyone said it was a shame. Fortyodd's pumpkins were the biggest in the world, but even with his friend Fiftytimes' help, he couldn't budge them an inch, let alone take them to the show! Still, he knew one thing — his grandfather would have been proud of him!

THE GOOD GOBLIN

WRITTEN BY CANDY WALLACE

Deep in the heart of a great forest, a long way away and a long time ago, lived a gang of goblins. Most of them were just like goblins everywhere — horrible. Small goblins attended school to learn how to be nasty. Soon they were taking exams in Telling Lies, Cheating, General Nastiness 1 and 2, Sneering and Loathing. The goblins who were better at doing things with their hands took Pinching, Punching and Stealing Things. If a goblin passed all his exams he got a Certificate in Nastiness and became a fully qualified goblin.

One of them, however, didn't quite fit in. His name was Pookie and he never managed to pass a single exam. When Question 1 said, "Describe, in not more than one hundred words, how you would steal a little girl's birthday cake," he wrote, "Well, actually I wouldn't do that because it's not really an awfully nice thing to do."

Question 4 said, "How would you make someone feel really miserable? Would you a. laugh at their skinny legs, b. trip them up, or c. give them a cuddle?" Pookie wrote, "Give them a cuddle," and got nought out of twenty.

The goblins used to go out on stealing expeditions. You know the sort of thing, making off with one sock so someone spends the next week trying to find it and ends up with not one matching pair. Or sneaking into a little boy's bedroom and taking his favourite toy. All the other goblins had given up on Pookie. They left him behind on these outings because as fast as they were stealing things, Pookie was taking them back. Once they returned and found he'd washed all their nicely grimy clothes and put them out to dry in the sunshine. He was absolutely impossible.

They tried taking him to the goblin doctor. "Can you give Pookie some medicine to make him nastier?" they asked.

"Well, young goblin," said the doctor to Pookie gravely, "I'm afraid this medicine is going to taste nice, but unless a medicine tastes nice, it won't do you any good at all. You'll have to be brave and take it every day." Pookie said the doctor was very kind and promised to follow his instructions.

A week later the goblins went to visit Pookie to see if he had become any nastier

"We're off to rip holes in shopping bags so all the food falls out!" they said to him, temptingly. "You'll enjoy that won't you, Pookie?"

"It's very good of you to invite me," replied Pookie, "but I promised a blackbird I'd help her make her nest today. I'm most frightfully sorry." And off he went, whistling a happy tune.

Nothing seemed to work. It was time to try something drastic.

"We'll go and ask the wizard to sort him out!" they cried. "He's the only one who can make Pookie nasty!"

Sure enough, in a cave near the forest lived an old wizard called Woozle. Woozle had a terrible temper and usually threw things at the goblins when they came near. But many's the time the goblins had seen him chanting and mixing strange potions. They saw him turn a snail into a teapot and a rabbit into a toothbrush. Changing a nice goblin into a nasty goblin should be a piece of cake for a clever wizard like him.

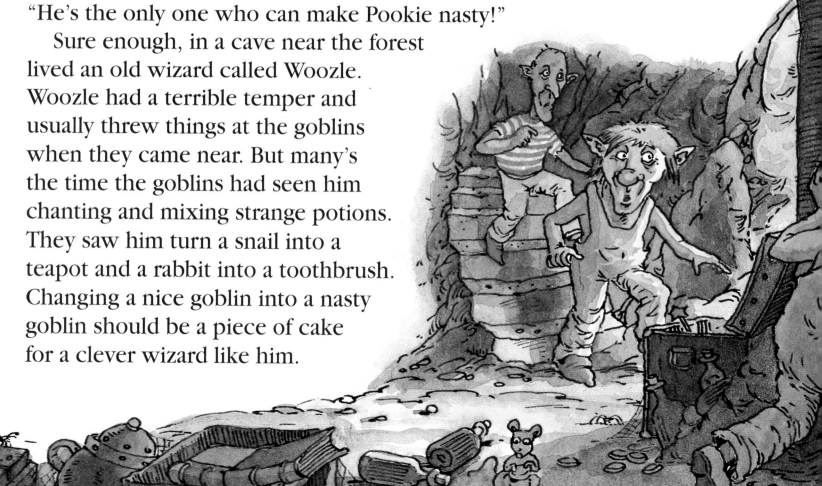

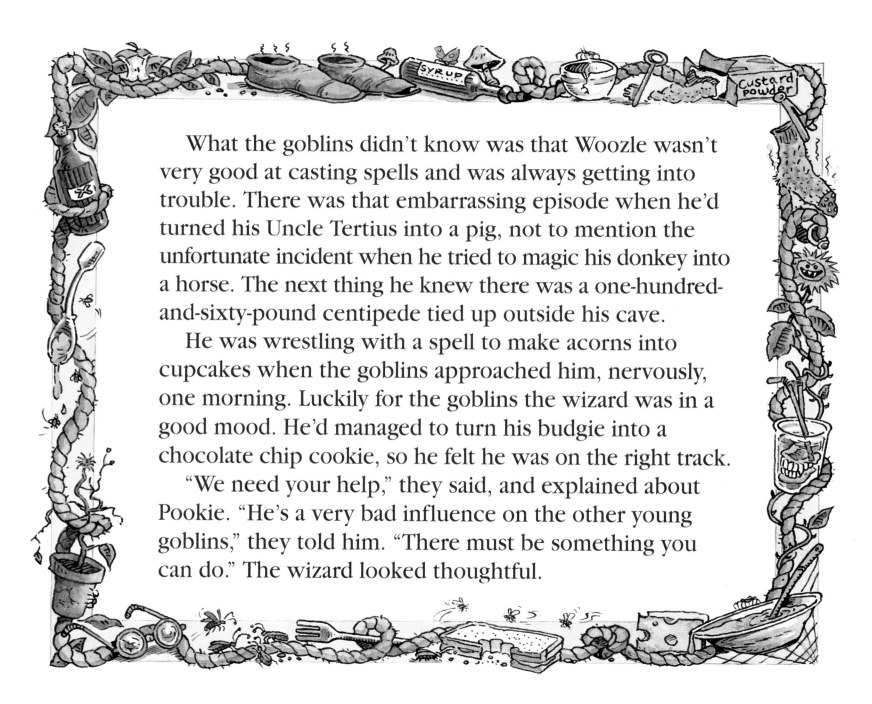

What the goblins didn't know was that Woozle wasn't very good at casting spells and was always getting into trouble. There was that embarrassing episode when he'd turned his Uncle Tertius into a pig, not to mention the unfortunate incident when he tried to magic his donkey into a horse. The next thing he knew there was a one-hundred-and-sixty-pound centipede tied up outside his cave.

He was wrestling with a spell to make acorns into cupcakes when the goblins approached him, nervously, one morning. Luckily for the goblins the wizard was in a good mood. He'd managed to turn his budgie into a chocolate chip cookie, so he felt he was on the right track.

"We need your help," they said, and explained about Pookie. "He's a very bad influence on the other young goblins," they told him. "There must be something you can do." The wizard looked thoughtful.

This was certainly a challenge for a wizard of genius and creative brilliance such as himself.

"All right, I'll do it," said Woozle. "I'll come over tomorrow with one of my magic potions. I'm sure it will be the simplest of matters to transform this poor, deluded young goblin into a fine, unpleasant young goblin. Leave it to me!"

The next day, all the goblins gathered together in a clearing to wait for the wizard's arrival. Pookie strolled along too, curious as to why everyone was so excited. Then he noticed they were all sniggering and pointing at him and he began to feel rather uncomfortable.

At last, the wizard arrived on foot. He was going to come on his centipede, but had changed his mind. It was a very obliging centipede and much better tempered than the donkey had been, but Woozle felt rather seasick whenever he tried to ride on him. It must have been all those legs.

So, when he arrived, the wizard was rather tired. He sat down on a rock puffing and blowing and coughing.

"I've ... brought ... the ... potion," he wheezed and wiped his brow. Reaching into his pocket he took out a little bottle with bright yellow liquid in it. "Where is the goblin in question?"

Instantly, Pookie knew it was him. He found himself pushed forwards by the other goblins. The wizard drew a chalk circle around Pookie and asked all the other goblins to stand around him and hold hands. Then he sprinkled the yellow mixture around the chalk circle.

Woozle took out a pair of wire spectacles and balanced them on his nose. Then he pulled out a tattered piece of paper covered in scribbles.

"Er, yes now, here it is, er, ah yes — here is nice where should be nasty, change this situation fasty!" The wizard took his specs off and coughed nervously. "Poetry was never my strong point," he apologised.

Nevertheless, he felt pleased. He looked at Pookie hopefully for signs of a sneer. But Pookie wasn't looking at him. Pookie was looking at all the other goblins. They were dancing towards the wizard, hand-in-hand.

"Thanks most awfully for coming to see us!" said one. "Have a nice cup of tea before you go," cried another.

"Do forgive us," said the Chief Goblin. "I'm afraid we can't stay, we simply must dash and help some old ladies cross the road. Good morning to you!"

The goblins skipped off happily down the path, pausing only to pick daisies and wave at passing butterflies.

Pookie and the wizard were left, staring in astonishment. They looked at each other and gulped.

"That was a very good spell, Mr Wizard," said Pookie at last. "You must be the cleverest wizard in the whole world."

Woozle put his spectacles away. He thought it was a good spell to finish his wizard career with. It was time to take up gardening.

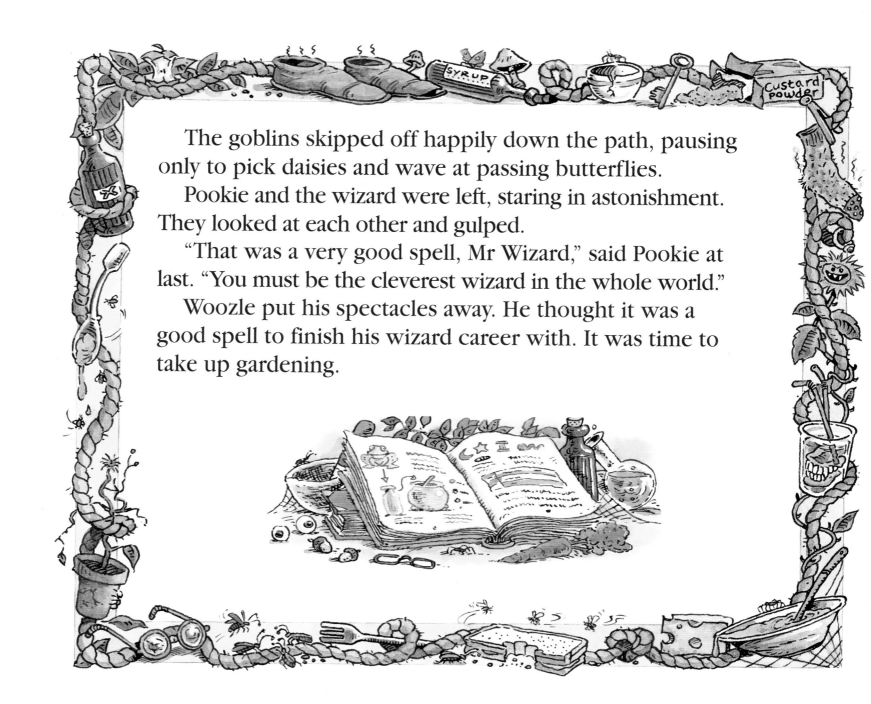

GNOME IMPROVEMENTS

WRITTEN BY CLAIRE STEEDEN

In a small garden centre, in a town not far from here, lived a gnome called George. At night, when it was dark and everyone had gone home, George and the rest of his gnome friends played on the swings and slides there and even swam in the pond. They all had lots of fun but were careful that nobody saw them move, hurrying back to their positions before it got light.

One morning, George overheard Sam, the owner, talking to Sarah, who worked there part-time.

"The garden gnomes don't seem to be selling well this year. I don't understand it, they've always been so popular," said Sam.

"Maybe they're too expensive. Why don't we put them on sale?" replied Sarah.

"That's a good idea. Could you paint a sign saying 'All gnomes half price'?" asked Sam.

"O.K. I'll do it this afternoon," said Sarah.

George was listening nearby. He felt worried all day, and that night he called a meeting to tell the others what he had overheard.

"That's terrible," cried Grace. "If we all get sold to different people we'll never see each other again."

"I don't want to be sold. I want to stay here with all of you," sobbed Gloria. "What are we going to do?" asked Gilbert. They all stood there thinking hard.

"We could run away," suggested Gladys.

"But where would we go? We've never been outside the garden centre," said Gerald. "Don't worry," said George. "I think I've got a good idea."

George had watched while Sarah had painted the sale sign. She had used paints and brushes kept in one of the garden sheds.

"Come with me and I'll tell you my plan," said George.

All the gnomes followed George to the shed. "Once we are on sale tomorrow lots of people will want to buy us. They like plain red and white gnomes in their gardens. But if we paint each other in lots of bright colours and patterns we'll look so awful that nobody will want us," explained George.

"That's a brilliant idea," cried Gladys, and all the others agreed. They could hardly wait to get started.

They pulled the shed door open and went inside. George climbed up an old wooden ladder and switched the light on.

One by one they opened the tins of paint. Throughout the night they had great fun painting each other in the brightest colours and most outrageous patterns they could think of. George had an orange hat with purple spots, lime green hair, a red and yellow striped jacket, blue trousers with silver stars and the brightest pair of pink boots you have ever seen! The rest of the gnomes looked just as dreadful. As they stood looking at each other, they started to laugh.

"We look awful," cried Grace.

"Nobody will want us in their garden," chuckled Gloria.

"I think we all look marvellous," said Gladys. "Let's just hope nobody else does!"

It was daylight when they finished clearing up — nearly time for Sam and Sarah to arrive for work. They just had time to get to their places and stand still before Sam and Sarah walked through the gate.

Sam took one look at the gnomes and let out a shriek.

"Aarghh, what's happened to the gnomes? We'll never sell them looking like that!"

George winked at the others.

"Some kids must have got in last night and mucked about. But look at the colours they've used! Even at half price nobody will buy them," said Sarah. "Come on, let's have a cup of tea."

All day long the customers remarked on how funny the gnomes looked.

"What a sight. I wouldn't have one in my garden if they were giving them away," said one man.

Then just before closing time an old lady came through the gate.

"Oh my," she cried when she saw the gnomes. "How wonderful! I've got a couple of gnomes in my garden but none as splendid as these."

"You mean you *like* them, madam?" asked Sam.

"Like them? I love them," she replied. "But which one shall I choose?"

On hearing this all the gnomes started to panic. Which one would she buy and take away with her?

"I can't decide," she sighed. "They're all so funny."

"They're half price in our sale, madam," said Sam. "Maybe you'd like more than one."

"What a splendid idea," she said. "In fact, I'll take them all. I can't do much gardening any more so I haven't got many flowers. These gnomes will add a splash of colour and make the garden look more cheerful."

"All of them? Are you sure?" asked Sam.

"Quite sure. It'll be money well spent," replied the lady. Sam took the lady's address so that they could be delivered. Sarah packed them into a big box and put them into the van.

On the way, George whispered to the others, "I don't want to leave the garden centre, but at least we're all together."

When they arrived Sarah carried the box to the front door and rang the bell.

"Oh good. I was hoping you'd be here before dark. I can't wait to put them in the garden," said the old lady.

Sarah carried them through to the back garden. When she had gone the lady carefully unpacked them one by one. When they were all unwrapped she said,

"My name is Daisy. Welcome to my home. It won't be as lonely now with all of you to talk to. It's just a shame you can't talk back."

Daisy put the gnomes around her lovely little garden. When she had finished she stood back to look at them. "My, you are colourful. You certainly brighten up my garden."

As it was getting dark, Daisy went inside and drew the curtains. After a while the gnomes started to whisper to each other.

"What a pretty garden," said Gilbert.

"There's a pond and a swing," said George. "It's probably for her grandchildren."

The other gnomes in the garden introduced themselves, and soon they were all chatting like old friends.

"I think we're going to be very happy living here," said Gladys, smiling.

When Daisy's friends saw the gnomes they wanted some too, so Sarah started to paint the new gnomes at the garden centre. They sold so quickly she could not paint them fast enough. Sam was pleased as business had never been so good, and it was all because of the friendly gnomes who wanted to stay together.

MONGO THE MONSTER

WRITTEN BY CLAIRE STEEDEN

It was eight o'clock, time for Katie to go to bed. She put on her pyjamas and went into the bathroom to brush her teeth. She watched herself in the mirror and started to pull funny faces, which made her giggle.

"What are you up to in there?" called her dad.

"Oh, nothing. Just brushing my teeth," Katie answered.

"Well, hurry up if you want a story," said Dad.

Katie wiped all the froth off her face and ran into her bedroom.

"About time," laughed Dad. "Which story shall we read tonight?"

"Mongo the Monster, please," said Katie.

"Oh, not again. Can't we have a different one?" moaned Dad.

"But it's my favourite," pleaded Katie.

Katie loved monsters. She had lots of monster books and toys and a huge poster of funny looking monsters on her wall. Katie thought the biggest one looked like Mongo in her story book.

Katie snuggled down and listened to her dad until he finished the story. As she lay there looking at her poster, wishing it was real and she could join the fun, she felt a little drowsy. She closed her eyes, and suddenly, she was standing by one of the trees in the poster and could hear the monsters talking.

"Has everybody arrived yet?" she heard Mongo ask, as he stomped around the forest clearing.

"I think so," answered a little monster.

Katie watched from behind a tree as the most amazing monsters appeared. They looked just like the ones she had seen in the story. They were very noisy, stomping about and making the funniest sounds. All the monsters turned to face Mongo.

"Hello, everybody. Welcome to our Monster Competition. I hope you are all ready for some monster fun! Let's start with our first game. Take your places, everyone, for the Monster Muscle Game."

With that they all cheered and formed a long line behind a huge rock. Katie could not help laughing at them because they were so funny. They wobbled about making strange noises. One of them kept jumping high into the air.

"Boing!" called Mongo. "I know you're excited, but could you stand still for one minute?"

The monsters laughed as Boing turned a deep red.

Katie could not believe her eyes when the first monster lifted the huge rock high above its head and threw it into the air. Within seconds it landed by the tree, narrowly missing Katie's head.

"Help!" she cried.

"What was that? Who's there?" asked Mongo.

"It's me," replied Katie creeping out from where she was hiding.

"Look at that!" bellowed Boing.

"What a funny looking creature," laughed Fang.

"It's all arms and legs," giggled Roly.

"What is it?" asked Boggle.

"What do you mean?" replied Katie. "I'm a little girl, my name is Katie and I don't look half as funny as you!"

"Pleased to meet you," said Mongo. "Where did you come from?"

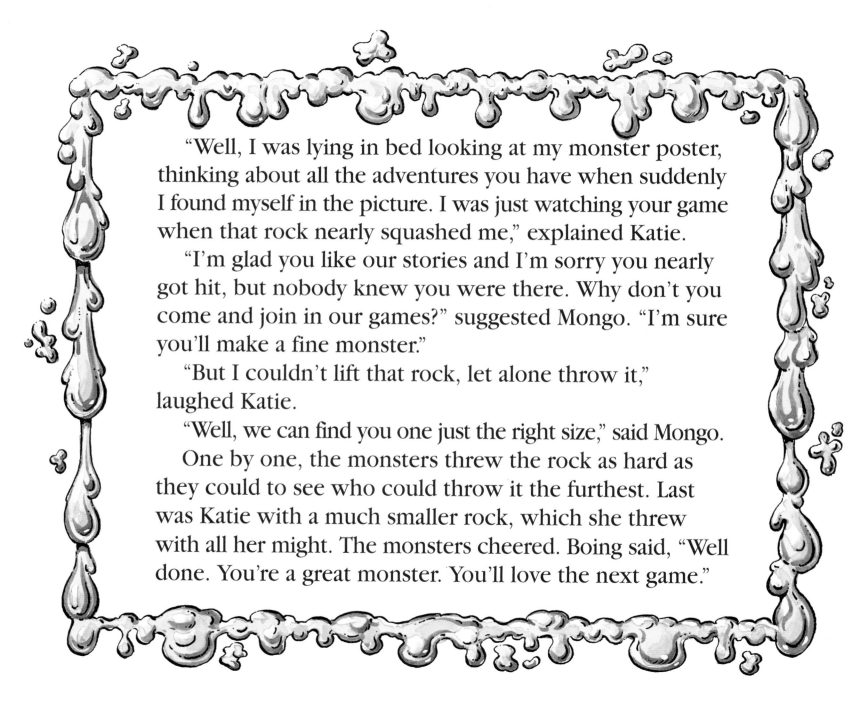

"Well, I was lying in bed looking at my monster poster, thinking about all the adventures you have when suddenly I found myself in the picture. I was just watching your game when that rock nearly squashed me," explained Katie.

"I'm glad you like our stories and I'm sorry you nearly got hit, but nobody knew you were there. Why don't you come and join in our games?" suggested Mongo. "I'm sure you'll make a fine monster."

"But I couldn't lift that rock, let alone throw it," laughed Katie.

"Well, we can find you one just the right size," said Mongo.

One by one, the monsters threw the rock as hard as they could to see who could throw it the furthest. Last was Katie with a much smaller rock, which she threw with all her might. The monsters cheered. Boing said, "Well done. You're a great monster. You'll love the next game."

All the monsters, including Katie, had to stand in the stickiest mud, and make a set of footprints. Then they each had to guess which set belonged to which monster. It was great fun, but they all got in a terrible mess, which Katie particularly enjoyed.

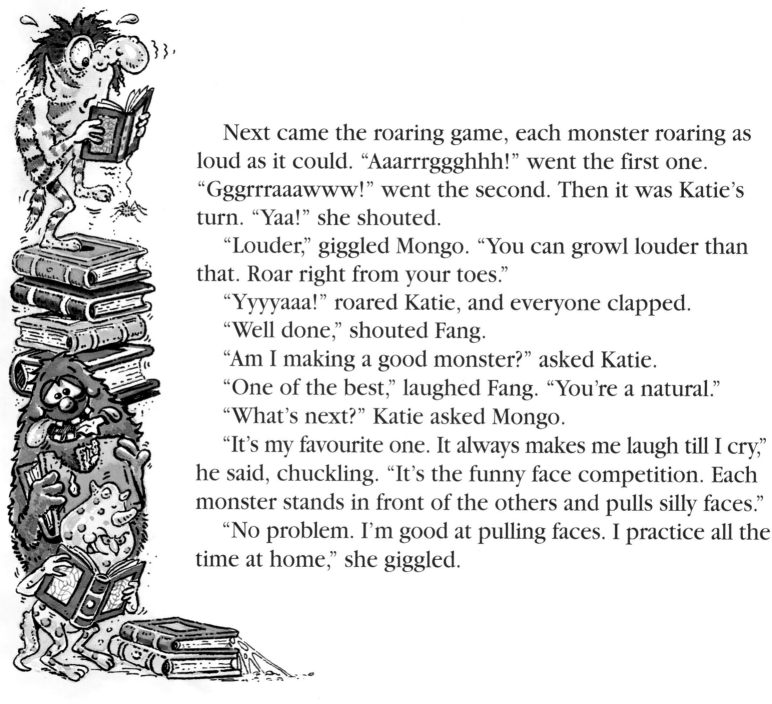

Next came the roaring game, each monster roaring as loud as it could. "Aaarrrggghhh!" went the first one. "Gggrrraaawww!" went the second. Then it was Katie's turn. "Yaa!" she shouted.

"Louder," giggled Mongo. "You can growl louder than that. Roar right from your toes."

"Yyyyaaa!" roared Katie, and everyone clapped.

"Well done," shouted Fang.

"Am I making a good monster?" asked Katie.

"One of the best," laughed Fang. "You're a natural."

"What's next?" Katie asked Mongo.

"It's my favourite one. It always makes me laugh till I cry," he said, chuckling. "It's the funny face competition. Each monster stands in front of the others and pulls silly faces."

"No problem. I'm good at pulling faces. I practice all the time at home," she giggled.

"Good. Then again you've got a funny face anyway. You've only got two eyes, one nose and a mouth. That's funny enough," said Mongo, and they both laughed.

They watched as the monsters pulled the most hilarious faces. They all laughed and laughed. But when it was Katie's turn they were all rolling on the ground and holding onto their tummies. They had never seen anything so funny.

After the last game the prizes were given out. Katie won first prize for the funny face game. Mongo pinned a gold star onto her pyjama jacket. Then they all danced and sang and had a great party.

Suddenly, Katie heard a loud ringing noise and turned to see where it was coming from. It was her alarm clock. She was lying in bed, all twisted up in her duvet.

"Oh! I don't want to be back here. I was enjoying my monster adventure," she said to herself. As she untangled

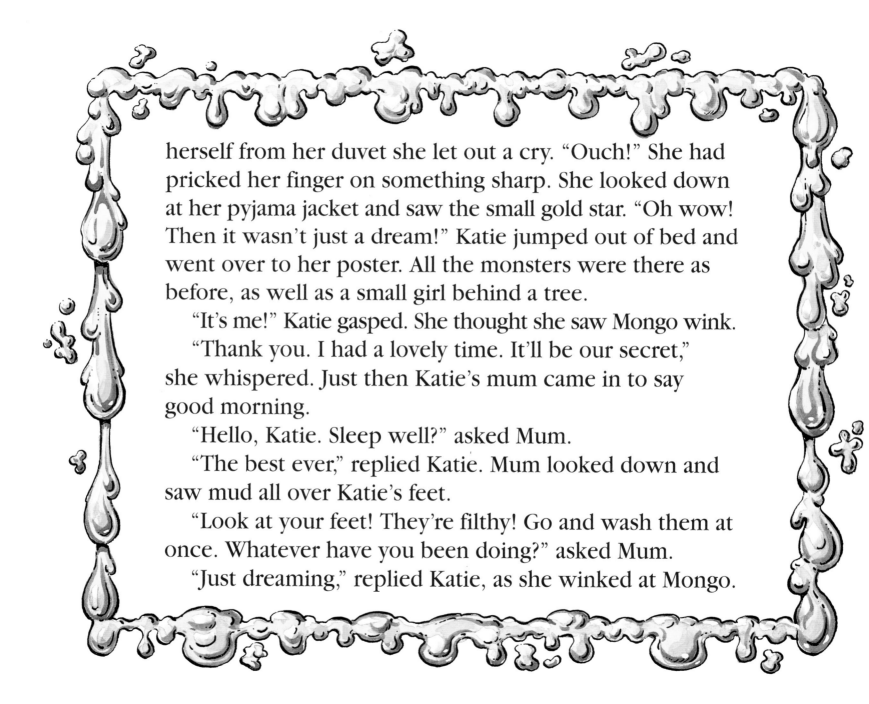

herself from her duvet she let out a cry. "Ouch!" She had pricked her finger on something sharp. She looked down at her pyjama jacket and saw the small gold star. "Oh wow! Then it wasn't just a dream!" Katie jumped out of bed and went over to her poster. All the monsters were there as before, as well as a small girl behind a tree.

"It's me!" Katie gasped. She thought she saw Mongo wink.

"Thank you. I had a lovely time. It'll be our secret," she whispered. Just then Katie's mum came in to say good morning.

"Hello, Katie. Sleep well?" asked Mum.

"The best ever," replied Katie. Mum looked down and saw mud all over Katie's feet.

"Look at your feet! They're filthy! Go and wash them at once. Whatever have you been doing?" asked Mum.

"Just dreaming," replied Katie, as she winked at Mongo.

BOTTOM OF THE GARDEN

WRITTEN BY CANDY WALLACE

Did you know there are probably fairies living at the bottom of your garden? It's the perfect place, with lots of tangly weeds, upturned flowerpots and old trees with handy holes in the trunk. And people seldom visit the bottom of their gardens. "I'm going to dig a nice vegetable patch down there this spring," they say, but they never do.

There was once a very old house that had been empty for years, so the entire garden was as wild as a jungle.

The lawn had been neat, short and bright green. Now the grass was so high it waved to you in the breeze and was tangled with wild flowers, nettles and prickly brambles that crept along the ground.

It all looked neglected and unloved to the human eye. But it was full of life — butterflies loved the wild flowers, little dormice nested in the grass, birds loved all the juicy worms and grubs to be had and, though you couldn't see them, the garden was the home of some other little creatures, too.

Until, that is, the new owners moved in.

One fine morning, a great big van and a red car drew up outside the old house and stopped. Out of the car scrambled a little girl and her parents.

The grown-ups started to move furniture and boxes into the house from the van, while the little girl, whose name was Lucy, decided to explore. It was just about the most exciting thing in the world to move to this lovely old house with its big garden surrounded by a wall. And Dad had promised her a swing! She walked around the side of the house to look at the garden and gasped when she saw the overgrown chaos. She sat down on a crumbling step, put her chin in her hands and tried to imagine it all tidied up with her swing in the corner.

"Excuse me," said a tiny voice. Lucy sat up straight and blinked. That was the trouble with daydreaming, you imagined all kinds of strange things.

"I'm up here," said the little voice again. "On the bird table."

Lucy squinted and rubbed her eyes. There seemed to be a very tiny person with flower petals on her head, sitting on the rickety bird table and swinging her legs.

She looked very like a picture of a fairy in one of Lucy's books. But of course, she couldn't be, because there were no such things as fairies.

"Are you lot moving in?" said the voice, "because this is our garden and we don't want it spoiled by people with big boots and spades and lawnmowers and weedkillers…"

Lucy blinked again. "Yes, we are," she replied. "Are you really a fairy? How very exciting! Wait here a minute and I'll fetch my mum and dad — they'll never believe me!"

"No point," said the little fairy. "Grown-ups can't see or hear fairies. Only children. Sorry."

"How can you live here?" asked Lucy. "It's horrible!"

The fairy looked cross.

"Most of us live either in the flowerpots, or the molehills or in the tree trunks or in old birds' nests. They're very cosy — I'm moving into one myself soon."

"Lucy!" called Dad, as he opened the back door and came into the garden. "Don't you worry about your swing. I'll soon knock this garden into shape." He beamed at her. "I'm going to clear the whole garden and lay a new lawn. I thought your swing could go over in that corner." With that he went back into the house to help the removal men.

Lucy turned around to see the fairy sitting on her shoulder, looking miserable.

"This is terrible," said the fairy. "This garden has been our home for years. All our best friends are here, the butterflies, birds, dormice and bees. We'll all have to find somewhere else to live. But goodness knows where."

As Lucy listened, little fairy figures hopped down from twigs and flowers, clambered out from under toadstools and popped their heads over the top of cracked flowerpots.

"Can you help us?" asked one.

"All the other gardens are spick and span around here. Where will we go?" said another.

Lucy's mother called to her from the house. It was time to sort out her new bedroom.

"I expect I dreamed all this, because I don't believe in fairies," said Lucy. "But if I didn't and you really are fairies and this garden really is your home, I promise I'll think of something to help you. I promise!" And with that she jumped up and ran into the house.

Over the next week or so, everyone worked really hard to clean the house. There was no time to clear the garden. Until one day, when a new garden shed and a shiny new set of gardening tools were delivered.

"I can't wait to start on this garden!" said Dad rubbing his hands with glee. "You'll soon have your swing up, Lucy!" and off he went to look at his new shed.

Lucy felt terrible. She still hadn't thought of a plan to save the fairies! If she didn't come up with something soon, they'd be homeless, and all the other creatures too!

She sat in her bedroom, gazing out at the garden and watching a fairy collecting cobwebs outside her window. A butterfly fluttered by and settled on the window ledge.

"I know!" cried Lucy suddenly. "I know just what to do!"
That evening, Lucy ate her tea with her mum and dad.
"Dad," she said, in between mouthfuls of toast. "I've had
a lovely idea for the garden."

"Don't talk to me about the garden," said Dad, gloomily. "It's going to take me forever to tidy it. It took me all day just to clear a corner for the shed."

"Well, I've had an idea," replied Lucy. "Why don't we leave the bottom half as a wildlife garden? Then the lovely wild flowers and all the butterflies and birds and — er — other little creatures — will still have a home!"

"That's a nice idea, Lucy," said Mum. Dad cheered up immediately. Only half the work to do!

So that's what they did. When Dad decided to make a pond in the wildlife garden that summer, only Lucy, sitting on her new swing, could see dozens of tiny creatures diving off the lily pads into the water and rowing tiny apple leaf boats. Little frogs soon moved in and water boatmen and dragonflies, too. In fact, Lucy's wildlife garden teemed with life, some of which the grown-ups would never, ever see.

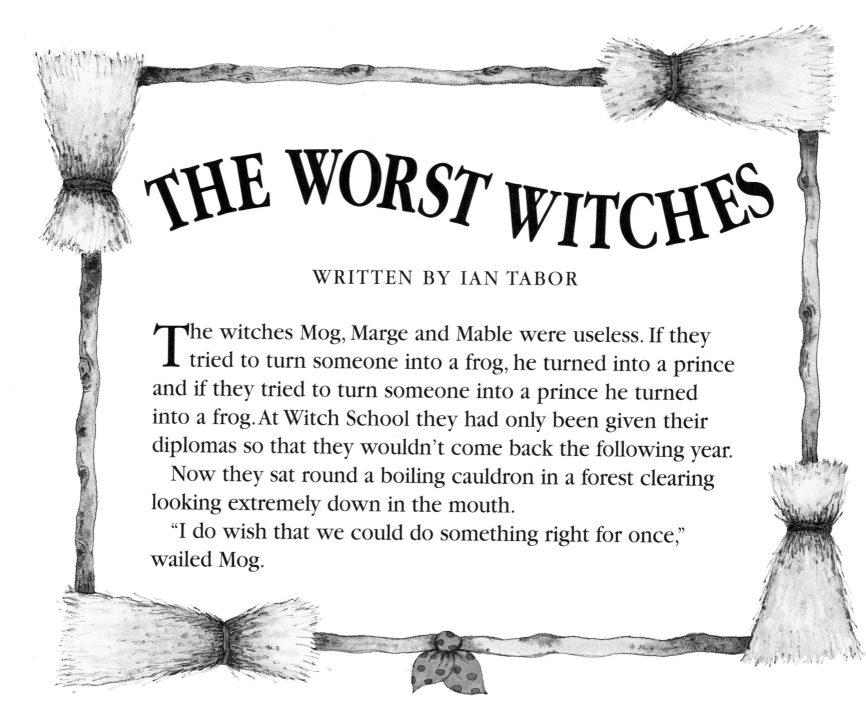

THE WORST WITCHES

WRITTEN BY IAN TABOR

The witches Mog, Marge and Mable were useless. If they tried to turn someone into a frog, he turned into a prince and if they tried to turn someone into a prince he turned into a frog. At Witch School they had only been given their diplomas so that they wouldn't come back the following year.

Now they sat round a boiling cauldron in a forest clearing looking extremely down in the mouth.

"I do wish that we could do something right for once," wailed Mog.

"The trouble is," said Marge, "almost everyone has heard how useless we are. Nobody in their right mind would employ us."

"Hey, listen to this," said Mable letting out a cackle. "DRAGON HOLDS KING TO RANSOM. A mad fire-breathing dragon is rampaging through the land, burning all trees before him. The dragon, known simply as Inferno, has said that he will only stop when the king gives him his daughter's hand in marriage. The king has refused and has called on all the brave knights in the kingdom to slay the dragon."

"Ooh!" exclaimed Mog. "We haven't had a dragon in the area for ages. What fun!"

"Not if he's burning down all of our trees it isn't!" said Marge.

"Well if you ask me," said Mable, "this is our chance to

show everyone that we're not just three useless old witches. We must stop the dragon, then we'll be heroines."

"But how?"

"Good question. Tell you what, why don't we have a think over a bowl of my nice soup?" And giving the cauldron one final stir Mable ladled the thick, green soup into three bowls.

"What exactly is in this? asked Marge, peering cautiously into her bowl, which was boiling and bubbling.

"Oh a little bit of this and a little bit of that," replied Mable mysteriously. "It's actually a new recipe that I've just made up."

The three witches sipped their soup, trying to think of a way to destroy the evil dragon.

"What's that?" asked Mog, looking up from her bowl of soup.

"What's what?" asked Marge.

"That sound. It's a flap, flap, flapping sort of a noise," Mog said, nervously.

"I can hear it as well," said Mable. "But where's it coming from?"

The noise was getting louder and louder. Suddenly Mog let out a piercing scream and pointed to the sky.

Marge and Mable followed her warty finger and there, above them, was the dragon.

"Run!" screamed Mog. "Run before we're fried!" In a mad panic they tried to run away from the monster but all they succeeded in doing was running into each other. Their bowls of soup went flying through the air and landed in the forest. Mog, Marge and Mable ended up in a jumbled heap on the ground.

The dragon swooped down letting out a scorching jet of fire. The witches screamed, but it was too late. Just as the flame was about to reach them and turn them into cinders the three witches fainted.

When Mog woke up she couldn't believe her eyes. The forest was just a smouldering lump of charcoal, all that is, except for three trees.

"Marge! Mable! Wake up!" she cried, poking the other two. "We didn't get burnt. We're alive."

The other two sat up, blinking in disbelief.

"And look," said Mog, pointing to the unharmed trees. "How do you think they survived?"

"It's a miracle!" exclaimed Mable.

"Close," said Marge. "It was your soup, Mable. Look. There's one of our soup bowls at the bottom of each tree. It might not be all that wonderful for eating," Marge said with a smile, "but your soup makes things fire-proof. You're a genius, Mable!"

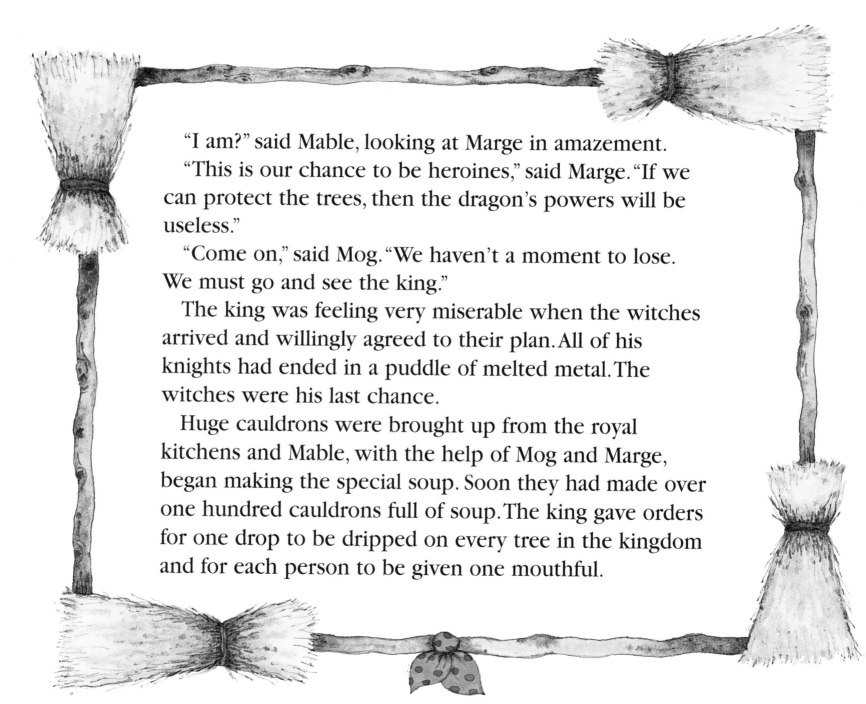

"I am?" said Mable, looking at Marge in amazement.

"This is our chance to be heroines," said Marge. "If we can protect the trees, then the dragon's powers will be useless."

"Come on," said Mog. "We haven't a moment to lose. We must go and see the king."

The king was feeling very miserable when the witches arrived and willingly agreed to their plan. All of his knights had ended in a puddle of melted metal. The witches were his last chance.

Huge cauldrons were brought up from the royal kitchens and Mable, with the help of Mog and Marge, began making the special soup. Soon they had made over one hundred cauldrons full of soup. The king gave orders for one drop to be dripped on every tree in the kingdom and for each person to be given one mouthful.

The next time the dragon came he got quite a surprise. He huffed and he puffed but he couldn't get even one small tree to catch alight. In the end he gave up and went back to his lair cursing the witches. The king was overjoyed.

"Well done! Well done indeed!" he exclaimed. "Not only have you saved all the trees in the kingdom, but my daughter will not have to marry that evil dragon. You are now my official royal witches."

Mog, Marge and Mable grinned in delight. Perhaps they weren't so useless after all.

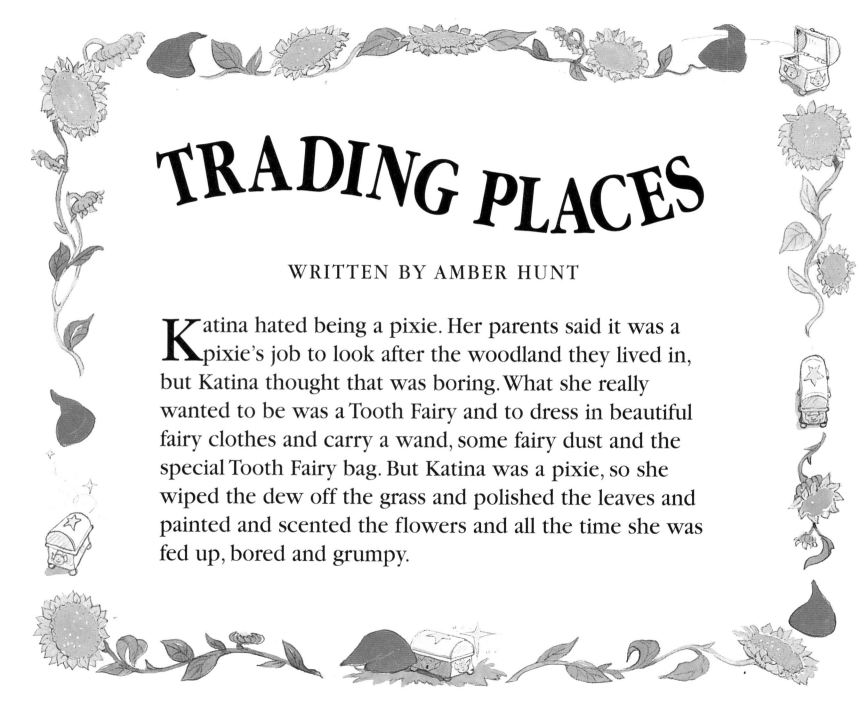

TRADING PLACES

WRITTEN BY AMBER HUNT

Katina hated being a pixie. Her parents said it was a pixie's job to look after the woodland they lived in, but Katina thought that was boring. What she really wanted to be was a Tooth Fairy and to dress in beautiful fairy clothes and carry a wand, some fairy dust and the special Tooth Fairy bag. But Katina was a pixie, so she wiped the dew off the grass and polished the leaves and painted and scented the flowers and all the time she was fed up, bored and grumpy.

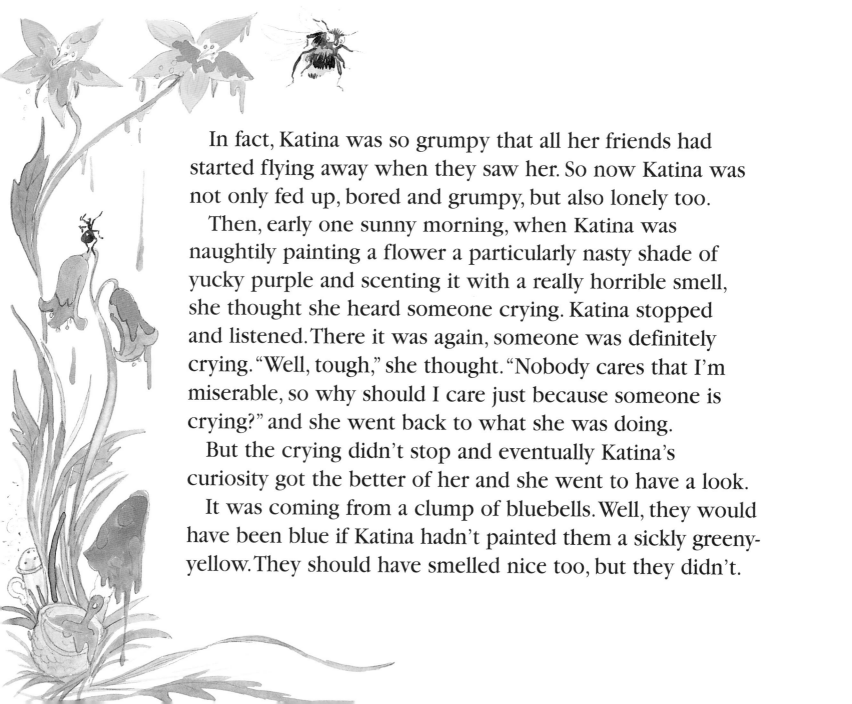

In fact, Katina was so grumpy that all her friends had started flying away when they saw her. So now Katina was not only fed up, bored and grumpy, but also lonely too.

Then, early one sunny morning, when Katina was naughtily painting a flower a particularly nasty shade of yucky purple and scenting it with a really horrible smell, she thought she heard someone crying. Katina stopped and listened. There it was again, someone was definitely crying. "Well, tough," she thought. "Nobody cares that I'm miserable, so why should I care just because someone is crying?" and she went back to what she was doing.

But the crying didn't stop and eventually Katina's curiosity got the better of her and she went to have a look.

It was coming from a clump of bluebells. Well, they would have been blue if Katina hadn't painted them a sickly greeny-yellow. They should have smelled nice too, but they didn't.

Katina tip-toed up to the smelly clump of greeny-yellow bells and peeped through. There behind them was… a Tooth Fairy!

"Gosh," said Katina. "A Tooth Fairy! Why are you crying?"

"Because I'm upset, stupid," snapped the Tooth Fairy.

"Oh well, fine," said Katina, "if that's how you feel, you can jolly well go on crying," and she went to fly off.

"No wait," said the fairy. "I'm sorry, I'm not usually rude. It's just that I've sprained my wing and I can't fly." Turning round she showed Katina her hurt wing.

"Oh," said Katina. "What are you going to do?"

"I don't know," sniffed the fairy. "I'm supposed to be visiting a little girl and we never let children down. But there's only a short time left before the little girl wakes up. She'll be so disappointed if her tooth is still there and there's no coin." The fairy started crying again.

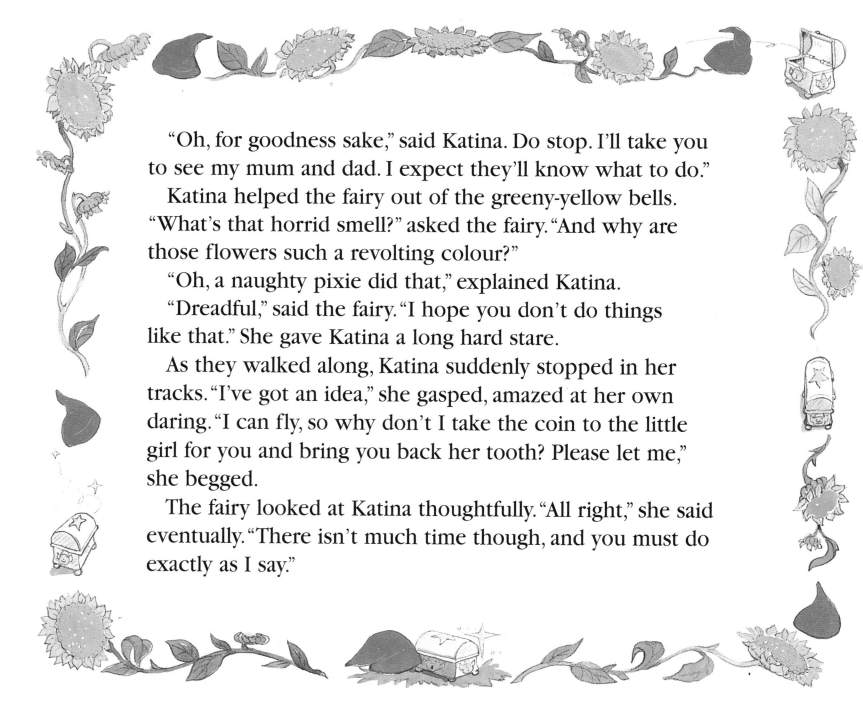

"Oh, for goodness sake," said Katina. Do stop. I'll take you to see my mum and dad. I expect they'll know what to do."

Katina helped the fairy out of the greeny-yellow bells. "What's that horrid smell?" asked the fairy. "And why are those flowers such a revolting colour?"

"Oh, a naughty pixie did that," explained Katina.

"Dreadful," said the fairy. "I hope you don't do things like that." She gave Katina a long hard stare.

As they walked along, Katina suddenly stopped in her tracks. "I've got an idea," she gasped, amazed at her own daring. "I can fly, so why don't I take the coin to the little girl for you and bring you back her tooth? Please let me," she begged.

The fairy looked at Katina thoughtfully. "All right," she said eventually. "There isn't much time though, and you must do exactly as I say."

She gave Katina precise instructions and made Katina repeat them back to her three times before she was satisfied. Finally, she gave Katina the special Tooth Fairy bag and sent her on her way.

Katina flew through the woodland bursting with joy. If she did this well, perhaps she would be allowed to become a Tooth Fairy one day.

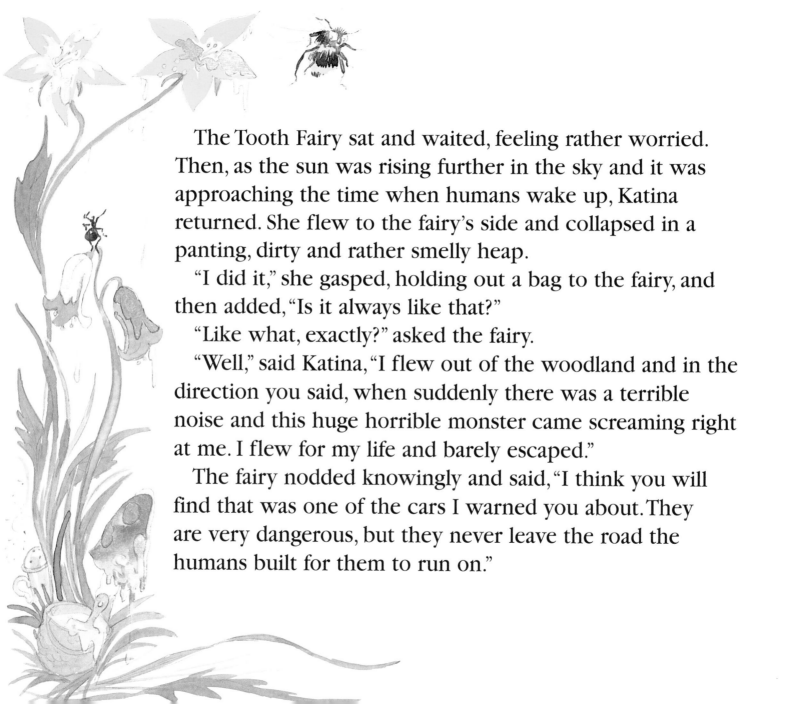

The Tooth Fairy sat and waited, feeling rather worried. Then, as the sun was rising further in the sky and it was approaching the time when humans wake up, Katina returned. She flew to the fairy's side and collapsed in a panting, dirty and rather smelly heap.

"I did it," she gasped, holding out a bag to the fairy, and then added, "Is it always like that?"

"Like what, exactly?" asked the fairy.

"Well," said Katina, "I flew out of the woodland and in the direction you said, when suddenly there was a terrible noise and this huge horrible monster came screaming right at me. I flew for my life and barely escaped."

The fairy nodded knowingly and said, "I think you will find that was one of the cars I warned you about. They are very dangerous, but they never leave the road the humans built for them to run on."

"Oh," said Katina, impressed by the fairy's knowledge. "Then I was chased by a big hairy monster with enormous eyes, massive fangs and hot evil smelling breath."

The fairy laughed.

"That was a dog. They are friendly and mostly they just want to play, but you have to be careful that you don't accidentally get squashed by them."

"After that," went on Katina, "I was chased by another, smaller monster. This one had big green eyes, sharp teeth and claws and it hissed at me. I had to hide in a smelly hill near the little girl's house, until it went away."

"Ah," sighed the fairy, "that was a cat. You have to be careful with cats. Sometimes they just want to play, but sometimes they can be very spiteful. You were wise to hide, although I suspect that what you hid in was called a compost heap. You really do smell quite unpleasant you know."

"Thanks a lot," sniffed Katina.

"You know," the Tooth Fairy went on, "since you've done so well the Grand Fairy Committee might consider allowing you to attend the Tooth Fairy School."

Katina smiled. "No thank you," she said. "I thought I wanted to be a Tooth Fairy, but after today, I've decided I'm very happy being a pixie.

"And no more nasty coloured flowers with horrible smells?" asked the fairy.

"Ah," said Katina, "you knew. No," she promised, "and I won't be grumpy any more either."

The fairy nodded, pleased, and gave Katina a big hug. Then, arm in arm, they went off through the woodland. The Tooth Fairy's wing soon recovered and she became the best of friends with Katina, who kept her little patch of woodland spotless.

A DREAM COME TRUE

WRITTEN BY GEOFF COWAN

What has huge claws and teeth, a long scaly body and tail, breathes fire and likes ice-cream? Answer: a dragon with a problem!

And that's why Smoky was fed-up. Now you may be forgiven for thinking dragons are horrible, fearsome, fiery creatures who do no good to anyone. But you'd be wrong. At least, you would be in the case of Smoky and all the other dragons who lived on the small, volcanic island of Dragonia.

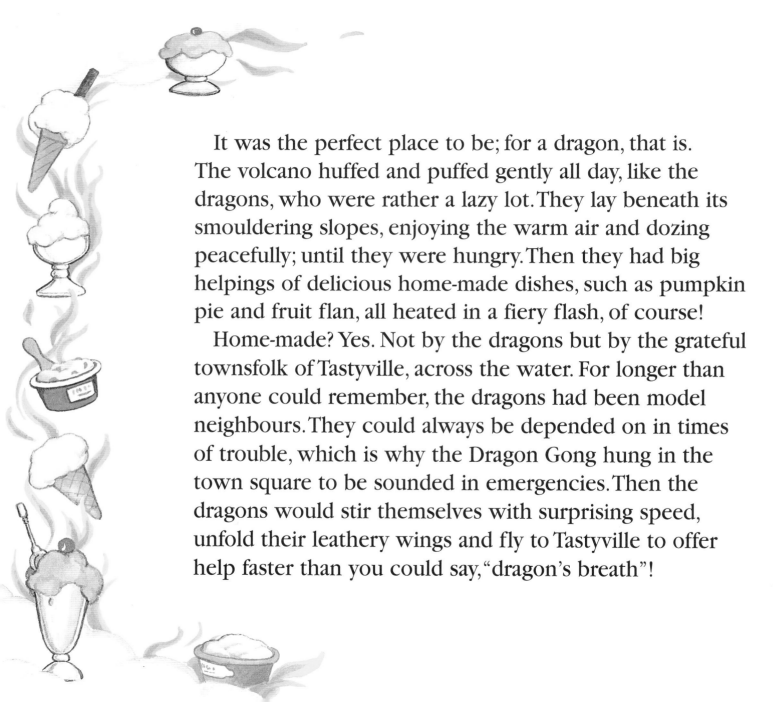

It was the perfect place to be; for a dragon, that is. The volcano huffed and puffed gently all day, like the dragons, who were rather a lazy lot. They lay beneath its smouldering slopes, enjoying the warm air and dozing peacefully; until they were hungry. Then they had big helpings of delicious home-made dishes, such as pumpkin pie and fruit flan, all heated in a fiery flash, of course!

Home-made? Yes. Not by the dragons but by the grateful townsfolk of Tastyville, across the water. For longer than anyone could remember, the dragons had been model neighbours. They could always be depended on in times of trouble, which is why the Dragon Gong hung in the town square to be sounded in emergencies. Then the dragons would stir themselves with surprising speed, unfold their leathery wings and fly to Tastyville to offer help faster than you could say, "dragon's breath"!

Whether it was to drive away invaders long ago, or in more recent times, just to fire up the blacksmith's forge on a wet morning, it didn't matter. The dragons would have a go at anything. They were very handy do-gooders to know. In return, the people of Tastyville fed them with all sorts of tasty treats. Apart from one important exception — ice-cream. The fame of the Tastyville Ice-Cream Factory knew no limits, save the shores of Dragonia. After all, how could such a fire-spouting bunch of dragons possibly eat ice-cold ice-cream? There would be meltdown the moment their burning breath settled on it.

Which is why Smoky dreamt of nothing else; ice-cream was the only food he couldn't have, which made him want it all the more. That and the fact that he was the only dragon ever to have eaten any!

What have dragons and elephants in common? Answer: long memories. After all, people say that elephants never forget and neither had Smoky. He had hardly hatched from his shell on that distant day when his mum returned from good-deed-doing in Tastyville with a tub of ice-cream for him.

Smoky had been too tiny then to breathe fire. So he'd lapped up the scrummy, fabulous, frozen delight, which now, sadly, he could only dream about.

Then one winter something happened that would make Smoky's dreams come true. It became known as the Coldest Winter. Tastyville shivered beneath the thickest snow anyone had ever known. Everything froze, even the sea in the harbour. So the mayor went to sound the Dragon Gong but couldn't find it under a snowdrift. Luckily, Smoky was practising some stunt-flying nearby. He saw the mayor waving frantically and went to find out what was wrong.

"If the sea-ice doesn't melt, ships won't get through with food for the town," explained the mayor.

"No food for Tastyville means none for us, either," thought Smoky, gloomily.

"We've tried dropping rocks on the ice but it won't even crack!" the mayor went on. "You must help us!"

"Stay cool," replied Smoky, blushing as he realised that wasn't the best thing to say. He quickly added, "I mean, don't get steamed up!" He decided that wasn't right either and became quite tongue-tied. But the mayor knew Smoky had something helpful in mind and watched the dragon wing its way back to Dragonia.

"I'll be back!" roared Smoky, through a cloud of scorching flame.

When he returned, he was not alone. The wintry sky was filled with beating wings. Not a single dragon stayed behind on Dragonia. Wrapping up warmly, the excited townsfolk hurried to the harbour to watch in wonder as the fiery flock hovered over the frozen sea.

"If anyone can melt the sea-ice, we're hot favourites!" bellowed Smoky.

Every dragon began to blast the ice with burning breath. So great was the heat that a golden red glow filled the sky. The snow over Tastyville dripped away and the townsfolk bathed in the warmth.

But the ice didn't melt; not at first. It was so thick, it stubbornly withstood the flame-throwing dragons.

"Breathe harder," rasped Smoky, a hot dryness in his throat.

More flames, more roaring, raging fire until, at last, less ice. First, the surface turned to water. Then the rest seemed to give up and melt all of a sudden. The harbour was open at last.

Even as the thankful people of Tastyville cheered, a ship sailed closer, bringing much-needed fresh food.

Everyone jumped up and down, and danced and sang for joy. Everyone, that is, except for Smoky. He lay wearily at the harbourside and seemed unable to move.

"What's wrong?" asked the worried mayor. "Are you ill? Do you need a doctor?"

"No, just… ice-cream!" whispered Smoky, his eyes half-closed.

"Ice-cream?!" gasped the mayor. "But what use is that to a dragon?"

All the same, a big tub of it was fetched from the factory and placed near Smoky. Everyone waited anxiously as he slowly scooped some up on the tip of his tongue.

"Amazing! It hasn't melted!" cried the mayor. "I don't understand!"

Smoky smiled blissfully as he swallowed the cold, creamy mix. It was the most delicious thing he had ever tasted. Slipping easily down his dry throat, it soothed the soreness from so much fire.

"It's simple," he said quietly. "I am so puffed out, that I'm not breathing hard enough to melt the ice-cream. If I just remember to breathe very gently indeed, I can eat all I want!"

Since then, Smoky has flown to the ice-cream factory once a week for a king-sized cornet or two, and only the odd one ever melts before it reaches his mouth!

So now what has huge claws and teeth, a long scaly body and tail, breathes fire and eats ice-cream? Answer: one very happy dragon!

THE SMALLEST GIANT

WRITTEN BY DAVE KING

Albert the Giant had a big problem. Or rather, he had a little problem that was, in fact, a big problem! And if all that sounds a trifle confusing, imagine how poor Albert felt.

Albert's problem was this: he wasn't a very big giant. Now, if you or I were to look at Albert, we would definitely say he was a big giant. Certainly, if you were to invite him round for tea at your house, you would soon see how big Albert was when he couldn't get in through the front door — in fact, he'd probably be taller than your entire house.

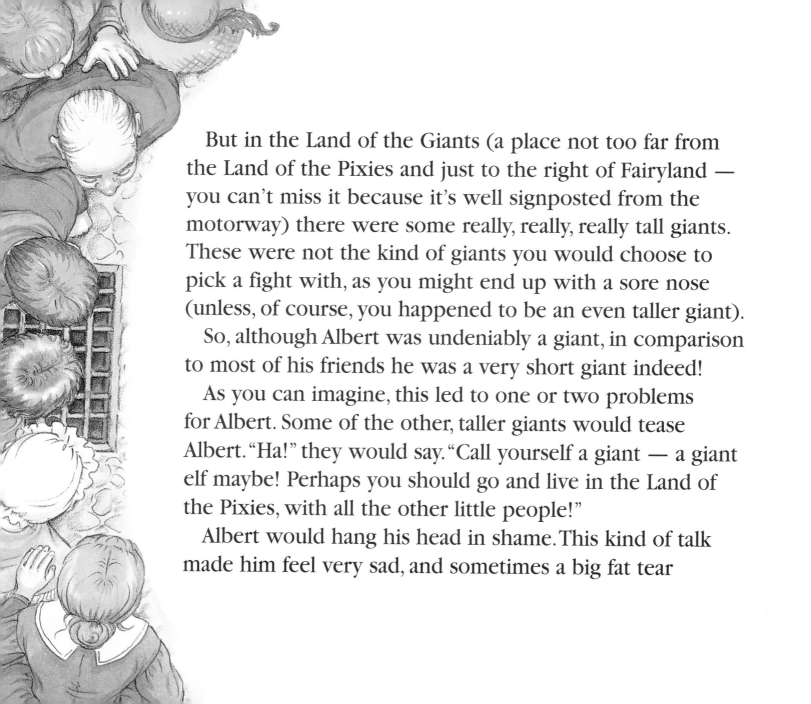

But in the Land of the Giants (a place not too far from the Land of the Pixies and just to the right of Fairyland — you can't miss it because it's well signposted from the motorway) there were some really, really, really tall giants. These were not the kind of giants you would choose to pick a fight with, as you might end up with a sore nose (unless, of course, you happened to be an even taller giant).

So, although Albert was undeniably a giant, in comparison to most of his friends he was a very short giant indeed!

As you can imagine, this led to one or two problems for Albert. Some of the other, taller giants would tease Albert. "Ha!" they would say. "Call yourself a giant — a giant elf maybe! Perhaps you should go and live in the Land of the Pixies, with all the other little people!"

Albert would hang his head in shame. This kind of talk made him feel very sad, and sometimes a big fat tear would roll down his cheek. He wished he could be the same size as all the others and he had tried all sorts of things to make himself grow. He had even visited a wise old witch in Fairyland, but the spell she gave him just made his nose grow longer and longer, so he'd had to go back and get the spell reversed. But generally speaking, he was a happy giant, and he did his best to keep cheerful about things.

One day, Albert was sitting at home reading a copy of *Gnomes and Gardens* magazine — a publication that delved into the lives and homes of gnomes, elves, pixies, fairies, sprites and all manner of little, magical people. It was a favourite of Albert's, as reading about people smaller than himself usually made him feel really rather tall. Suddenly, he heard a dreadful commotion coming from outside his house. He rushed over to the window only to discover that his view was blocked by masses of other giants, out in the street.

He tore open the front door and tried to push his way through the crowd. "Excuse me!" he shouted. "What's going on? What are you all looking at?"

But it was no use. The crowd of giants, with their backs to Albert, were cheering too loudly. If you've ever heard one giant shout, you're probably deaf by now! Just imagine how loud a whole crowd of giants can be… loud enough to knock your next door neighbour's wig off, I'll guarantee!

Whatever was happening in the middle of the street, it was making the giants very excited. Albert didn't want to miss all the fun, so he dropped down onto his hands and knees and began to weave his way between the legs of the crowd. After a while he reached the front of the crowd, and through the tangle of legs he could see a big crowd on the other side of the street, equally excited and equally noisy.

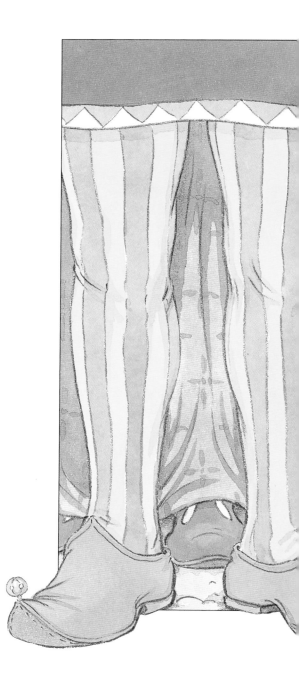

Albert tilted his head to one side and listened. Just above the roar of the crowd he could hear something. It sounded like… it was… yes, Albert could definitely hear the sound of a trumpet! He wiggled through the rest of the crowd and stood up. The sight that greeted him as he looked down the street was a grand one. Smiling regally from inside his royal carriage, the King of the Giants was leading a grand parade through the streets of the town. It was the tenth anniversary of the King's coronation, and he was leading the way to an enormous party being held in his honour. The King was a real sight to see, bedecked in jewels from top to toe and with a gleaming crown. "I bet that cost him a few week's pocket money!" Albert thought, as he stared at the King's finery.

Now it just so happened that for the past few weeks, King Bill the Second had been on a diet. He was rather fond of food, to say the least.

It was nothing for him to eat two chickens, a raspberry trifle, a plate of chips, three doughnuts and a chocolate fudge cake all in one go. And that was just for breakfast!

"You must get some exercise, and lose some weight!" Doctor Harold, the Royal Physician had told him. "And if I might suggest…" the doctor continued, holding up a videotape, "I've just brought out my own exercise tape, *Lose Weight the Harold Way!* Only nine pounds, ninety nine pence to you, Sire!"

Even after the doctor had been thrown out into the street, the medical man's words rang true in the King's ears as he looked down at his flabby waist. He decided to go on a diet, cutting down on all the cakes and sweets that he liked to munch on during his favourite television shows, eating more sensibly and even taking a little, just a little, mind… exercise.

And so it was that just as King Bill drew near to where Albert was standing, he gave one of his little royal waves (which he was frightfully good at), and as he did so, one of his most beautiful — and horrendously expensive — rings slid off his newly slender finger, landing with a clink in the road and rolling several yards before sliding straight down a drain grating!

"It's disappeared, your Highness," said one of the King's guards, scratching his head and peering down the drain. "We'll never get it out of there!"

The King let out a terrible shriek. "My ring!" he cried. "Oh woe! Truly my ring is lost for ever!" Albert thought the King was over-reacting a bit. He watched as the other giants took turns to try and pull the grate up from the drain. They huffed and they puffed, but try as they might, it wouldn't budge. "There will be no more festivities until my ring is found," declared the King. Albert decided it was time to help out. "Um… excuse me, I'm sorry to bother you, your Majesty, but I think I might be able to help!" Albert said politely (he was a particularly polite giant, you see).

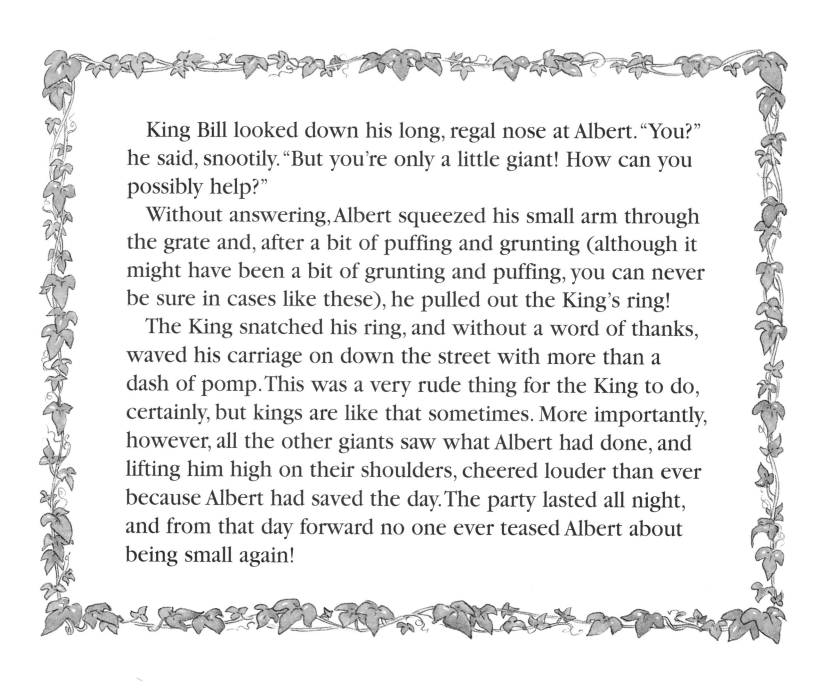

King Bill looked down his long, regal nose at Albert. "You?" he said, snootily. "But you're only a little giant! How can you possibly help?"

Without answering, Albert squeezed his small arm through the grate and, after a bit of puffing and grunting (although it might have been a bit of grunting and puffing, you can never be sure in cases like these), he pulled out the King's ring!

The King snatched his ring, and without a word of thanks, waved his carriage on down the street with more than a dash of pomp. This was a very rude thing for the King to do, certainly, but kings are like that sometimes. More importantly, however, all the other giants saw what Albert had done, and lifting him high on their shoulders, cheered louder than ever because Albert had saved the day. The party lasted all night, and from that day forward no one ever teased Albert about being small again!